IMPOSTER

D0676177

C0000 002 636 302

Jill HathaWay
IMPOSTER

HarperCollins*Publishers*

First published in hardback in the USA by HarperCollins *Publishers* Inc. in 2013
First published in Great Britain by HarperCollins *Children's Books* in 2013
HarperCollins *Children's Books* is a division of HarperCollins*Publishers* Ltd,
77-85 Fulham Palace Road, Hammersmith, London, W6 8JB.

www.harpercollins.co.uk

1
Imposter
Copyright © 2013 by Jill Hathaway
All rights reserved
ISBN 978-0-00-749030-1

Jill Hathaway asserts the moral right to be identified as the author of the work.

Printed and bound in England by Clays Ltd, St Ives plc.

Conditions of Sale
This book is sold subject to the condition that it shall not, by way of trade or
otherwise, be lent, re-sold, hired out or otherwise circulated without the
publisher's prior consent in any form, binding or cover other than that in which
it is published and without a similar condition including this condition being
imposed on the subsequent purchaser. All rights reserved.

MIX
Paper from
responsible sources
FSC
www.fsc.org   FSC˚ C007454

FSC™ is a non-profit international organisation established to promote
the responsible management of the world's forests. Products carrying the
FSC label are independently certified to assure consumers that they come
from forests that are managed to meet the social, economic and
ecological needs of present and future generations,
and other controlled sources.

Find out more about HarperCollins and the environment at
www.harpercollins.co.uk/green

For J, S, and F—
the men in my life

CHAPTER ONE

The dream always goes like this:

I'm in the passenger seat of a car, racing down the interstate. The smell of gasoline stings my nostrils. My lips are moving, and sound is coming out, but my words don't make any sense.

And I know what's going to happen, but there's nothing I can do about it.

The woman with white hair and death eyes is behind the wheel. She won't stop laughing. When I try to tell her to stop the car, that she's going to kill us all, my words are all backward and inside out and she just laughs and laughs. She turns her face toward me, and there are worms and spiders wriggling out of her mouth. I'm so distracted that I almost forget—

We're going to die.

There's a grinding noise, and we both look out the windshield at the same time. The road curves to the left, but we go straight, flying off the road, the headlights illuminating stalks of corn.

The tree comes out of nowhere.

The screams make my ears throb, but I can't cover them with my hands because they're holding the plastic container of gasoline.

An explosion of light and heat.
And then we are no more.

My limbs go rigid as I find myself awake. My mouth is open, but I'm unsure whether the screams stayed in the dream or followed me into my darkened bedroom. When the door pushes open and my sister, Mattie, pads inside, I know that I must have awakened her. My father, a pediatric surgeon with a huge surgery slated for tomorrow, must have his earplugs in. At least I didn't wake *him*.

Mattie lifts the covers, and I scoot over to make room for her. "Was it the dream again?" she whispers, and I turn to look at the ceiling. Mattie knows I dream of Zane's death, but she doesn't know that in the dream it's me dying. That I was actually with him when his psychotic mother crashed the car, killing them both instantly. That I was . . . inside him.

There is no technical term for what I am, what I can do. At least not that I know of. The moment Zane died, I was in his mind the way I've slid into the minds of so many others when I've touched something they've left an emotional imprint on. That night, I was purposely trying to get into Zane's head to locate my missing sister, so I tapped into him using one of his beloved Fitzgerald novels. People can leave bits of themselves on all sorts of things—jewelry, clothing, furniture, money. It all depends on what they're touching when they feel a surge of emotion.

I wasn't always able to slide. In fact, I was pretty normal until I turned twelve. That's when I started to slide. In one particularly upsetting episode, I was taking advantage of the fact that Billy Morgan was out of the classroom and hiding his Cubs pencil case behind the teacher's desk, and the next I found myself using a urinal in the boys' bathroom. It was pretty traumatic. Since then, I slide into others whenever I touch something with a strong emotional imprint. Sometimes I can stave it off by munching caffeine pills, trying to stay alert and focused, but most of the time I have no control. Only over the past year have I learned how to manage my power. There are still times, however, when I'm exhausted or distracted—and I just can't help it.

But Mattie doesn't know all this. All she knows is that my first love was killed in a horrific car accident six months ago and he keeps haunting my dreams. She reaches her arm across me and squeezes. She gets how dreams can seep out of your head into reality. She lost her two best friends around the same time that Zane died—one to murder and one to suicide. I imagine her dreams are as bloody as mine.

"It's only three thirty," I say, after peeking at my alarm clock. "Let's just go back to sleep."

Mattie nods, her eyelids already drooping. I watch her drift off, and then I roll over and stare out the window. Sometimes I can see my mother's face in the shine of the moon, but not tonight. The clouds are too thick.

The smell of bacon pulls me from my restless sleep. My father must have gotten up extra early to make us breakfast before he leaves for the hospital. I glance at the alarm clock. Not even six yet. Mattie's mouth is wide open, and she lets out these sporadic snores that sound like a little dog yipping. I roll out of bed without disturbing her and turn off my alarm clock.

Downstairs, my father stands at the kitchen counter with his back to me. His dark hair lifts in adorable little spikes. Though I know full well he's made Denver omelets enough times to be able to recite the process backward and forward, he traces his finger gently over an orange cookbook lying open before him.

It was my mother's.

I retreat into the front hallway and approach the kitchen again, shuffling my feet loudly so he can hear me coming. When I enter, I see that he's closed the cookbook and returned it to its home between the extra virgin olive oil and canisters of exotic spices.

"Good morning," he booms. "How did you sleep, Vee?"

I could tell him about my nightmare-riddled sleep, but I don't want to worry him before he goes in for a big surgery. He needs his mind clear when he works on the babies. He has to be able to forget about everything, including his girls at home.

"Fine," I say, plucking a piece of bacon that's been cooling on a paper towel and popping it into my mouth. The crispy meat melts into salty deliciousness against my tongue. "Yum." I grab another piece.

"Is Mattie awake yet?" he asks.

"Uh, no," I say. "I'll go get her."

Upstairs in my bedroom, I stand for a moment, hesitating. Mattie could get another half hour of sleep if I leave her alone. From the dark circles that are permanently under her eyes, I know she's been as sleepless as I have. Still, I'm sure she'll want to see Dad before he leaves for work. I bend down and squeeze her shoulder.

"Mattie," I say gently. "Breakfast. Dad made bacon."

She doesn't move.

I put my hand on her leg and shake. "Mattie!"

"What? What's wrong?" She bolts upright, staring at me with wide eyes. I wonder if she was dreaming of Sophie, lying motionless in a puddle of blood on her bed. Or Amber, sprawled on the football field with a hole in her head. Mattie's had horrifying luck with best friends lately. I don't blame her for being jumpy.

"Nothing, Mattie." I tousle her hair. "Breakfast."

Mattie is still shaking when we sit down at the table. My father has set out three placemats, three plates, three glasses. It's been a long time since there were four of us. It hardly even hurts anymore to look at the chair by the window, the one where she used to sit.

Under the table, I pull a tattered picture out of my pocket. My mother is young in the picture, smiling broadly at the camera, under the shadow of a sombrero. She and my father were on their honeymoon in Mexico when the picture was taken.

With my blond hair and blue eyes, everyone who knew her says I'm the spitting image of my mother. I push the photograph back into my pocket. I know it's dumb to carry it around, but ever since the horror of last fall, it makes me feel like she's with me. A little.

"So what are you doing today, Dad?" Mattie asks, grabbing a piece of toast and smearing some butter on it. I spear a forkful of eggs and lift them to my mouth.

"It's a case of polydactyly," he says. At our blank expressions, he goes on to explain, "The girl was born with an extra digit on her right hand. Today I'm going to remove it."

I put down my fork.

"I tried to explain to the parents that it would be best to wait until she's a little older," he says. "But they aren't comfortable living with the deformity. I can't say I blame them, exactly. People can be cruel. . . ."

"The parents are willing to risk surgery just to get rid of an extra finger?" Mattie asks, voicing my own question. It seems wrong to cut a baby just to make her fit into a mold that society is more comfortable with. They're uneasy with her appearance, so they'll *make* her fit in. I wonder what would have happened if I'd been diagnosed with my sliding condition in the womb. Would my parents have thought I was a freak? If there were an operation to make me normal, would they have requested it? I suspect my mom wouldn't have because I think she was able to slide, too. She regularly suffered fainting spells. I bet, just like me, she found herself sucked into other people's heads, other people's lives. Too bad she died before I was ever able to ask her. Now I'll never know. Whenever I try to broach the subject with my father, he starts talking about something else.

My father doesn't believe that I can slide. I tried to tell him when it started happening, but he sent me to a shrink who said I was just trying to get attention after my mother died. I've tried hard to forgive him for that, for thinking I was lying, for pushing me away when I needed him the most. But sometimes the anger creeps up inside me and I just have to get away from him.

"The parents want to take care of the problem before she's old enough to remember it," my father explains.

"I'm going to take a shower," I say, pushing my chair back from the table. My father and sister watch me grab my plate and glass, which I rinse off and put into the dishwasher before trudging upstairs. My sleepless night has started to weigh on me, and I wish I could just crawl back into bed.

Rollins, my best friend, will be here in a half hour, and that lifts my spirits a bit. He always knows what to say to cheer me up.

"You look like hell," Rollins says when I open the door of his old Nissan and slide in. He hands me a Styrofoam cup of coffee. "Decaf," he says. "Just like you asked. I don't know how you drink that shit."

After taking a sip of the steaming liquid, I lift my middle finger. "Excuse me if I haven't been sleeping well. I thought cutting the caffeine might help."

His face goes serious. "The dreams again."

Unlike Mattie, Rollins knows what really happens in my dreams. That I'm reliving the moment of Zane's death. He knows what torture it is for me.

"Yup," I say, taking another sip. "In full Technicolor."

"Ugh, Vee. I'm sorry."

At that moment, the back door swings open and Mattie throws herself inside. The whole car fills up with her too-sweet perfume, and I start to gag. "Jesus, Mattie. Did you empty the bottle?"

"Hey," she snaps. "*Someone* hogged the shower, so I didn't get a chance to wash my hair this morning. Do you have any idea who that might have been?"

I give her a sheepish look. I kind of fell asleep a little between washing my hair and putting in the conditioner. Mattie woke me up by pounding on the door and shrieking that she was going to pee her pants if I didn't open up right away. The only way I was able to appease her was by letting her borrow my black scoop-neck sweater.

"Sorry," I mutter.

Rollins shifts the car into reverse and backs out of the driveway.

I let my gaze flit from house to house, lawn to lawn, as he maneuvers through our neighborhood, toward the school. Gone are the leaves that littered the lawns months ago, when I was in love with Zane. Snow has been here and melted away, leaving the grass shyly green, the way it is in April, with flowers starting to push up toward the sun. I wonder if I'm taking too long to get over the hurt of Zane's betrayal, the fact that he knew his mother wanted revenge on my family and let her move forward with her sick plan, even after he fell in love with me. Sometimes I wonder if he ever did really love me. Or if what I felt for him was true love. Because if it was, it just makes me really sad. I always thought that love was supposed to be this pure, renewing thing, but what Zane and I had turned out to be rotten on the inside.

Rollins's voice slices through my thoughts, bringing me back to the moment. He's got the White Stripes playing on the stereo, and the doors and floor of the car seem to vibrate with the sound.

"Did you hear what I said?"

"I'm sorry. What was it? Something about the radio?"

"I got the internship," Rollins says excitedly. "At KRNK, the university station? They want me from ten to two on Tuesday and Thursday nights. It's perfect because I'll be able to—" He stops himself midsentence and glances at Mattie in the rearview mirror. I know what he's worrying about: that he almost spilled his big secret, that he has to take care of his mother every night—make her food, give her baths, and even tuck her into bed. He needn't have stressed, though. I peek in the backseat, and Mattie is thoroughly consumed with her cell phone, probably texting Regina, a freshman on the cheerleading squad who Mattie's become close with in the last couple of months.

Rollins continues, "I'll still be able to work at Eternally Vinyl on the weekends."

"That's great," I say.

"Yeah. I'm starting tonight. You'll listen, right?"

"Of course," I say. "You need at least one listener for your big debut, right?"

Rollins reaches over and punches my shoulder playfully. I massage the place where he made contact and pout, pretending to be hurt. His eyes meet mine, and I hope he knows, despite my joking, that I would do anything for him. Ever since he pulled me out of a burning building last fall and confessed his feelings for me, there's been this growing *thing* between us. It's like neither of us wants to explore it just in case it ruins our friendship. And, truthfully, after the way my relationship with Zane ended, I'm not sure I can handle another heartbreak.

We pull into the school parking lot, and Mattie leaps from the backseat the minute Rollins cuts the engine. She's been hanging out with Rollins and me more since her best friends were killed, but when she's at school, she'd much rather be with the rest of the girls on the Pom squad. They all banded together closely after losing two of their cheerleaders, almost as if they're grasping for some sort of normalcy during such an insane year.

I hoist my backpack over my shoulder and follow Rollins across the parking lot. As soon as I step inside the school, I freeze. The place looks nothing like it did when I left yesterday. Pink and gold streamers are strewn everywhere. Across from the front entrance, there's a long, rectangular folding table. It, too, has been decorated with gold paper and pink balloons. Above it all hangs a sign that says IT'S THAT TIME AGAIN! BUY YOUR PROM TICKETS HERE!

Ugh. I totally forgot.

Mattie was yapping on and on last night about how prom tickets were going on sale today. She was all depressed because she was sure no one would ask her to the dance, which is totally ludicrous because not only is Mattie one of the most popular girls in the freshman class, but all the freshman guys are in love with her. Why wouldn't they be? She looks like Cheerleader Barbie.

I used to be like her, naive and wrapped up in the delusion that my reputation was everything, relying on my looks to garner attention. But then something happened my sophomore year that turned my perception of the popular kids on its head.

My best friend at the time, Samantha Phillips, and I both had a crush on the same guy: Scott Becker, the hottest football player in our class. I was the one he asked to Homecoming. And I said yes, even though I knew how much it would hurt Samantha. The night was going beautifully until I felt myself get woozy in the middle of the dance floor. Scott asked me if I wanted to sit down, and I nodded. By the time he pulled me down the steps to the boys' locker room, I had completely passed out. When I awoke, I found my skirt around my waist and Rollins punching Scott in the face. I never found out exactly what Scott was doing while I was unconscious, but I have a good idea.

After that, my so-called friends ostracized me. Samantha passed around a rumor that I did it with Scott (nicknamed Scotch after he threw up all over the dance floor) in the locker room. None of the cheerleaders would talk to me, so I dropped out. I dyed my hair pink in some sort of defiant gesture. It made me feel more like I was rejecting everyone instead of the other way around.

Since then, I've dyed my hair back to the original shade

that matches my sister's. I've even started talking to some of the cheerleaders again. But it's not the same. Once I saw behind the curtain, I couldn't go back to thinking that crowd was worth my time. But Rollins has been by my side through it all. Just as he is now.

"Look, Vee! It's that time again!" Rollins says, grabbing my arm in mock excitement.

"Oh, joy," I say, my face twisting into a grimace.

The long line of students clamoring to buy prom tickets is kind of surprising, really. I thought more people would be scrambling for dates at the last minute. But the way the guys are digging out their wallets and making small talk with one another while they wait makes me think that people have been obsessing about this stupid dance for weeks, if not months.

Prom.

Bah.

I'm about to push past the table and head to my locker when a familiar voice makes me freeze.

Scotch Becker.

He leans over the table, winking at Samantha, my ex–best friend, who is presiding over the money box. "Hey, Sam. What are you doing tonight? Want to go to the bonfire with me?"

Samantha bats her eyelashes. "I might be persuaded."

"Awesome. I'll talk to you at lunch," Scotch says, spinning away from the table and running smack into me. His breath stinks, like he ate an onion bagel for breakfast. Or maybe he just forgot to brush his teeth. It makes my stomach turn.

"Get off me, Vee," he says, leering. "You had your chance."

"Screw you," I spit.

"You wish," Scotch says.

I feel Rollins's hand on the small of my back. He leans down and whispers in my ear. "Come on, Vee. Let's go."

As we walk away, Rollins mutters, "Asshole."

CHAPTER TWO

Something strange happens during English class.

One minute, Mrs. Winger is at the board, scribbling the definition of *motif* onto the whiteboard, and the next . . . she isn't.

There's just nothing. It's not like I fell asleep. I can still feel myself there, but somehow I'm not anymore. I'm floating in a big sea of black. There are muffled noises, and every now and then I can make out a word or two. Time seems to speed up or slow down. Minutes pass, or an hour. I don't know. And then I'm back again, in the same chair, my notebook with a half-finished definition of *motif* written down in purple ink.

I look around me, wondering if anyone noticed anything odd. Across the room, Samantha is staring at me. Out of everyone, she would know if I was acting strangely. Before the Homecoming Debacle of Sophomore Year, we did everything together, from painting each other's toenails with zebra stripes to dancing to Lady Gaga on my bed.

She hasn't spoken to me since the fire during a party at her house last fall. Not even to thank me for trying to pull her out before she was consumed by the flames. Unable to drag her by myself, I fainted. Rollins was the one to save us both.

Now Samantha sits there staring at me, like she knows something weird happened but she can't quite put her finger on it. She takes a lock of her red hair and wraps it around her index finger again and again. Finally, she shrugs and goes back to her notes.

I look down at my hands.

They're shaking uncontrollably.

Attributing the whole incident to a lack of caffeine, I pick up my pen and finish copying down the notes on the board.

By third-period study hall, I am feeling positively drained. Caffeine withdrawal is no joke. My head is pounding, and I want a cup of coffee so badly I feel like every vein in my body is crying out.

I tuck myself into the back of the library and lay my head on the desk, shutting my eyes. I'm even able to get a few seconds of sweet rest before the librarian rudely awakens me, tapping her garish red fingernails on the desk.

"The library is not your bedroom," she says. "You need to keep your head up. If you don't have any work to do, find something to read."

I bite my tongue before saying something that would probably land me in detention, and watch her walk back to the front desk. Sighing, I stand, wander over to the magazine rack, and grab a *Sports Illustrated*. I paint a fake smile on my face for the librarian's benefit and head back to my desk.

For a few minutes, I turn the pages, not really seeing the pictures. The tiny black type swims in front of me. Before long, I feel my head bowing again. But this time I'm not falling asleep. This is different. I can feel something on the pages of the magazine, a force compelling me to give in. I am about to slide.

The walls of the gymnasium pop up around me. I'm slowly jogging beside Randall Fritz, a junior on the football team. Air pumps steadily in and out of my lungs. The person I've slid into opens his mouth: "Tonight is going to be insane."

Scotch again.

Ugh, only he would leave an emotional imprint on a tattered copy of a sports magazine. I briefly wonder what I did to piss off the universe so much that I'm forced to encounter this Neanderthal twice in one day. Though when I'm inside him, it's hard to smell his stink breath, so that's something.

I'm guessing Scotch is talking to Randall about the bonfire I overheard him mention this morning, the one he asked Samantha to attend with him. It's all anyone's been discussing this week. Not that I'm going.

"I know, dude. I'm stoked."

Before I can hear any more of their conversation, I am swiftly transported back into my own mind, which is kind of a relief. I don't need to hear Scotch and Randall talking about how wasted they're going to get tonight.

At lunchtime, I lie on the ground underneath the bleachers, waiting for Rollins. This is our private space, among the trash and the leaves that have blown under here since fall. It's not much, but it's better than sitting in the cafeteria that mysteriously always smells like cabbage, watching the jocks compete to see who can eat the most slices of greasy pepperoni pizza.

I hear footsteps and open one eye.

"I brought you something," Rollins says. He holds out a Mountain Dew.

"You're so evil," I say.

After a long internal debate, I rationalize that Mountain Dew isn't as bad as coffee, and I might just need the drink to get through the day. I unscrew the cap and take a long swig.

Wiping my mouth with the back of my hand, I say, "Thanks."

He shrugs. "Thought you might need it, the way you looked this morning."

"You know me too well. I actually slid into Scotch Becker during third period. Today has been made of suck."

Rollins looks at me with concern. He is the only person who knows that I can slide. When he found out, he was definitely freaked, especially when he learned that I'd slid into him while he was giving his wheelchair-bound mother a bath, but since he got over that he's been amazingly supportive. "Are you okay?"

"Yeah," I say. "I just overheard him talking to Randall Fritz. They were making plans for that bonfire tonight."

"How fascinating," Rollins says.

"Exactly," I reply. "So are you nervous for tonight?"

Rollins chews on his lip ring. "No."

"Bullshit," I say.

He sighs. "It's not that I'm *nervous*, per se. It's more that I'm apprehensive. What if no one calls in? What if I spend the whole night just talking to myself? What if I *suck*?"

I offer him a drink from my Mountain Dew. His fingers brush against mine as he takes it from me, and a shiver goes up my spine, as cliché as that may sound. It really, actually does. I pull my hand back, hoping he didn't notice.

"You know me too well," he says, handing the bottle back to me.

"It's true."

Dinner is my favorite—homemade pizza with green peppers on top.

I watch my father and Mattie bow their heads to pray. My sister's cross necklace, the one that used to be my mother's, reflects light from the old chandelier hanging above the table. My mother picked out the chandelier, along with most of our other furnishings, at a flea market.

I search for the comforting feeling of the picture of my mother that I stashed in my pocket this morning, but it's not there. I reach deeper. Nothing. After checking the other pocket with no luck, I start to worry. Did I drop it somewhere?

"So how was the operation?" Mattie asks when they're finished praying.

To my relief, my father doesn't go into detail, as he sometimes does when discussing a particularly interesting case. He takes his oath seriously and never tells us the names of his patients, but he usually can't resist raving about how well a surgery went or ranting about how a nurse nearly botched the whole thing.

"As well as could be expected," he says. "I just hope the parents made the right decision." I think about the baby recovering from the surgery. My heart clenches for her.

"How was school?" he asks.

Mattie cuts in before I can even say a word.

"I got terrible cramps during first period," Mattie moans dramatically. "I had to go to the nurse, and she gave me an Advil and let me lie down for a little bit."

My father looks a bit like he regrets asking. He turns to me. "How about you, Vee? Did you have a good day?"

I nod, taking a big bite of pizza. Hell if I'm going to tell them about the weird experience I had during English class today. Or about sliding into Scotch. I'm attributing both of those occurrences to caffeine withdrawal. Neither my father nor Mattie knows that, up until a few weeks ago, I was swallowing twenty to thirty caffeine pills a day, trying desperately to stay awake so I wouldn't slide.

"I learned what *motif* is," I offer.

My father bobs his head, looking almost like he'd rather hear about Mattie's period than about the literary terms I'm studying. "Good, good." He lifts his slice of pizza and takes a big bite.

"Hey, have either of you guys seen that old picture of Mom, the one where she's wearing a sombrero?"

Both of them shake their heads.

After that, we eat in silence.

Long after the dishes have been rinsed and loaded into the dishwasher, I'm sprawled on my bed. My alarm clock says it's three minutes past ten. Earlier this afternoon I found a dusty old radio in my father's study, and now I'm twisting the dial, looking for KRNK. All I hear is static. Spinning it the other way, I finally locate the right channel—and hear a familiar voice.

Rollins.

He's talking about the ridiculousness of prom—how dumb it is for guys to spend weeks of paychecks to fork out sixty bucks a ticket, not to mention a hundred on a tux and another twenty on a corsage. Some idiots even rent a limo for the occasion. It's a rant I've heard a million times. The corners of my mouth turn up into a smile. I close my eyes and sink into the familiarity of his voice, his words.

"My colleague Anna disagrees with me on this point," he says.

My eyes fly open. Who is Anna?

Rollins continues. "I mean, I get where she's coming

from. There's the whole romance aspect of it. You're supposed to make the girl feel like a princess and sh—crap. But the thing is, if you're really into someone, you shouldn't have to spend a ton of money to prove it. Why not just rent a couple of scary movies and make some popcorn?"

I grin. That's what we do every Friday night—watch horror movies and eat junk food. We call it Friday Night Fright. I can't help but wonder if there's some deeper meaning to his words. Is he trying to tell me something, hint that he still has feelings for me? Or is this all hypothetical? Just banter for his radio show?

I grab my pillow and hold it to my chest.

"Anyway, I'm sure you're all tired of listening to me go on and on. Instead, I'll play a song that, to me, screams true romance." I hear him clacking through CD cases, looking for the right one. "Here it is. 'Everlong' by Foo Fighters. Okay, all you naughty kids, staying up late on a school night. This is what a rock song should sound like."

As the opening chords rattle the old radio, I close my eyes. Is this song meant for me? This song about waiting and wishing and wanting someone for so long? Could Rollins still feel the same way about me that he did that night in October? Or has he met someone else, someone who is ready to love him back?

The music rolls over me, and a silly image pops into my head. Rollins, in a vintage tux, and me in a glittery black dress. We sway together to the music, moving too slowly for the fast song.

———

This dream is not like the others.

Instead of the passenger, I'm the driver. The steering wheel is hard and unwieldy beneath my grasp, and there's the distinct scent of vanilla in the air—the smell of the air freshener my sister put in my father's car when he started taking her for practice drives.

I'm not on the interstate like I usually am in my dreams. I'm on some strange country road I don't recognize. The gravel crunches beneath the tires. Cornfields race by, a blur of shadows in the night. For some reason, the car is going faster and faster. It takes me a minute to realize my foot is pressing hard on the accelerator.

The moonlight shining down, the detail on the wooden fence that pops up on the left, the sweet smell in the air—everything is too real. I try an experiment and yank the wheel to the right.

The car veers, and I feel my stomach lurch as inertia claims me. The car rolls into the ditch, but it doesn't stop there. I see a telephone pole in my peripheral vision, and when it slams into the side of the car, pain shoots through my arm and chest where the seat belt tightens. My head slams against the window, and everything goes black.

When I wake up, I search for the comfort of my room, my telescope, the old rocking chair that used to belong to my mother. Instead, all I see is the vanilla air freshener, dangling inches away from my face, spattered with blood.

I sit up, wincing at the pain that sears through my head. Shaking, I reach for the rearview mirror and adjust it so I can see myself. My face is pale in the moonlight, with rivulets of black-red blood snaking down.

It wasn't a dream.

This is really happening.

How the hell did I end up here? The last thing I remember is falling asleep, listening to Rollins's voice on the radio. How could I possibly have risen, unaware, snuck down the stairs and out the door, and climbed into my father's car?

It just doesn't make any sense.

Scrambling, I look around for my phone. If I was able to somehow get into the car and drive myself into the middle of nowhere, maybe I had the sense to grab it. But there's nothing in the center console or on the floor. I open the glove compartment and shuffle through my father's registration and insurance papers. Nothing.

I push open the door and stumble out into the chill that is Iowa on an April evening. The wind slices through my thin T-shirt. I duck my head into the car and grab a University of Iowa sweatshirt that my father tossed in the backseat at some point. It does little to warm me up, but it's better than nothing.

Where am I?

The gravel road seems to stretch on forever in both directions. In the sky, Ursa Minor shines brightly. The mama bear constellation. It makes me feel a little less alone. I turn around and see the glow of the city. I start walking down the road, heading toward the light. My mind races as I try to make sense of it all.

Strange occurrences certainly aren't new to me. I'm used to sliding into people unexpectedly and having to figure out who the hell I am and what I'm doing. But this is something else. This isn't sliding. I'm not in someone else's body. I'm in my own. It's almost like . . . someone else took over my body and forced me to steal my father's car and drive out into the country.

It's like someone else slid into me.

CHAPTER THREE

Eventually, the gravel road turns into a paved one, and a sign looms ahead.

Highway 6.

I seem to be a few miles south of town.

My vision goes fuzzy for a moment, and I have to hold out my hands to steady myself. Perhaps I lost too much blood in the accident. I take a few deep breaths and then, feeling better, I carry on. My bare feet, not up to the task of trudging mile after mile, have become numb. I wince, imagining what they'll feel like tomorrow.

I keep racking my brain, trying to figure out who could have slid into me—and why. Ever since I learned to steer people's actions during a slide, I've been wondering what happens to the original inhabitant of the bodies. Do they go somewhere else? Do they just kind of black out?

I remember this time I slid into my father when he was jogging. I was so surprised to find myself in his body that I lost my balance and caused him to trip and fall. He landed on the pavement hard. And then I slid back into my own body.

I ran downstairs to find my father limping in the front door, looking dazed. He pointed to his ankle and said he must have fainted during his run. One second he'd been finishing his lap around the block, and the next he collapsed on the street. Now I wonder if there was a point in between, when everything turned murky and strange. Like how I was in English today.

Is it possible that someone slid into me while I was asleep and brought me here? How could it be possible? I've never heard of anyone else with the ability to slide—and, trust me, I've spent plenty of time Googling. What's the likelihood of there being another slider out there? One with access to something I touched and left an imprint on? Because that's what it would take for someone to slide into me.

No. It's not possible. It has to be something else.

Something up ahead shines into my eyes. Headlights! I wave my hands over my head, praying that the yellow sweatshirt I'm wearing is bright enough to make me visible to the driver.

"Hey," I shout. "Help!"

The car slows down beside me, and I see that it's a cherry-red, vintage Mustang. The sight of it brings back sickening memories. I've ridden in a car just like this before—the night of the homecoming dance last year, to be precise.

26

My fears are confirmed when the driver rolls down the passenger-side window. Scotch Becker leans toward me. "What the hell are you doing out here, Vee?" He's not alone. In the backseat, Samantha Phillips is sprawled drunkenly singing the school fight song, her eyes half-closed. The pungent scent of alcohol wafts from the car.

"Need a ride?" Scotch asks, smirking.

All of a sudden, I flash back to last year's homecoming dance. Scotch has the same look on his face that he did when I awoke with my skirt around my waist—at least, until Rollins punched him.

I back away from the car, feeling like I'm going to puke. I turn and stumble into the ditch. Little spots swim before my eyes. I hear a car door open, and I panic. On instinct, I start to run, slipping into the maze of corn. I'm only vaguely aware of the husks slicing into my bare feet. I don't slow down.

"Vee!" Scotch calls. "Vee, are you insane? I'm not going to hurt you!"

I ignore the voice and keep going. All I know is that I'm stranded in the middle of nowhere with a boy who may or may not have tried to molest me last year. I'm bleeding and confused. I just want Scotch to go away.

"Stop!" I hear Scotch panting. His footsteps slow, and then cease. "I won't chase you. If you want to stay out here all night, fine. It's your choice."

My feet are killing me. I quit running and listen to myself breathe. Long, jagged mouthfuls of air. I look up at the sky and wish on the North Star that he will just leave.

"Crazy bitch," I hear him mutter, and then more footsteps, moving farther away. Before long, his car starts up. Scotch revs his engine a few times and then takes off. Relieved, I sigh and head back toward the road. His taillights become smaller and eventually disappear.

I start to walk toward town, forcing my feet to keep moving, even though each step is agony. I fix my gaze on the city lights ahead. My destination seems a million miles away, even though I know it can't be more than five. Still, that's an awfully long way to walk on bare feet in the middle of the night.

A few minutes pass, and I hear a car somewhere behind me. I turn and watch the headlights come closer. Shielding my eyes, I try to decide whether I should try to flag the person down. Scotch was bad enough. What if the next driver is a serial killer?

In the end, my feet win out, and I wave my arms to get the driver's attention. The car slows and stops beside me. It's a blue station wagon. There's a woman with a bun and kind eyes behind the steering wheel. She reaches for a button, and the window goes down.

"Do you need some help, sweetheart?" she asks.

I hesitate.

It seems like a terrible idea to get in a car with a stranger, but I'm pretty sure I could take this woman if it came down to it. She's at least sixty years old and looks like she'd weigh about a hundred pounds soaking wet. And there's just something about her that seems reassuring.

"I was in an accident," I explain. "Could you give me a ride into town?"

"Of course," she says, pressing another button. The doors unlock.

I pull open the door and sit in the passenger seat. Warm air from the heater blasts my face and legs, and all of a sudden I feel sleepy. I raise my fingers to my face, which is all sticky. Gross.

"Oh no. You're bleeding," the woman says. She reaches out hesitantly, as if to touch my forehead, but she stops before making contact.

"It's okay," I say. "My father's a doctor. He'll be able to fix me up. Besides, I think it's stopped bleeding."

She opens the glove compartment and takes out a package of Kleenex. "Why don't you press some of these on your cut, just to be sure?"

I grab a few tissues and hold them to my wound. "Thanks. I really appreciate you giving me a ride. What's your name?"

"Diane," she says, returning the package to the glove compartment. After looking over her shoulder, she pulls the car back onto the road.

"I'm Sylvia," I say.

She nods, keeping her eyes on the road.

We ride in silence for a bit. I start to doze.

Before long, we pull into my driveway. Every light in

my house is blazing. As I get out of the car, the door opens and my father's silhouette appears. He steps onto the porch in his slippers and robe. I know that I'm in deep trouble.

"Thanks again," I tell Diane.

"Anytime," she says.

I shut the door, and she pulls out of the driveway.

It is only then that I realize I never gave her directions to my house.

CHAPTER FOUR

Without a word, my father holds the door open for me. "Where the hell have you been?"

I stop and turn to face him. I haven't seen him this angry since the time he found out Mattie went to an all-night kegger instead of going to a movie.

"Do you know how worried I was? I called the police. They asked whether I wanted to report my car stolen. But—they wouldn't go out and look for you until you'd been gone for twenty-four hours."

I think of how mangled my father's car is and wince. "I'm sorry."

He crosses his arms. "I can't wait until you have kids of your own and you wake up to go to the bathroom in the middle of the night and realize one of your kids has snuck out of the house. And taken your car. Jesus, Vee, you don't even drive."

"Dad. I didn't sneak out."

"Then what happened?" he demands.

"Maybe we should sit down so I can explain," I say.

Sitting down might be a very good idea for this conversation.

He eyes me warily, then follows me into the living room. I fall onto the comfy plaid couch, and he perches at the edge of his recliner.

"Now. Tell me."

I take a deep breath, knowing how crazy my story is going to sound, even if I leave out any references to sliding.

"I fell asleep in my room, listening to the radio. When I woke up, I was driving. I thought it was a dream. But then I realized it was your car, and it was all real. That's when I . . . sort of lost control and crashed into a telephone pole."

"Oh. My. God." My father lifts his hand to his mouth.

"I'm really sorry, Dad. About the car, I mean. I don't know what—"

I stop talking when he rushes over and sweeps me into a hug.

"Vee. My baby. Are you all right? Are you hurt? Let me see you." He holds me at arm's length and looks me over. "Your head." He brushes my hair away from the gash and inspects it carefully. "You might need a stitch."

I wiggle out of his grasp. "It's okay, really. It's stopped bleeding."

My father stares. "So who drove you home?"

"This woman who happened to be driving by." I neglect to tell him the creepiest part, that she knew where I lived without any directions. He's already freaked out enough as it is. Besides, I was so out of it on the car ride home, it's possible I told her my address and don't remember.

"Sylvia," my dad says firmly. "You shouldn't have gotten into a car with a stranger. Why didn't you call me?"

"I didn't have my phone," I say weakly. "I didn't know what else to do."

"My God. I don't know what I would've done if you had been . . ." His voice trails off, and we avoid eye contact, each of us thinking about what could have happened.

"You're my heart," he whispers, and I'm startled to see that he's crying. I reach over and wipe away a tear that's trickled down by the side of his mouth.

"Don't worry, Dad. I'm okay."

He manages a shaky smile.

"Is it okay if I go up to bed now? I'm exhausted."

He kisses my forehead. "Of course, honey. Go get some rest."

I leave him alone on the couch. He doesn't follow me up to bed. That's good because I have no intention of resting right now. Not after the night I've had.

Upstairs, my phone is right where I left it, on my nightstand. I grab it and punch in Rollins's number. He answers before the phone even finishes its first ring. He sounds frenzied. "Vee! So glad you called. The show was so amazing. You listened, didn't you?"

"Yeah, you were really great. But I'm actually calling about something else . . ."

Rollins is suddenly all business. "What is it? What's wrong?"

I suppose I can't blame him for assuming the worst after the craziness I put him through six months ago. I called him one night, begging him to help me save my sister from the killer who'd already murdered one of her friends.

"I'm okay," I say, making my voice calm, trying to reassure him. "I just . . . kind of . . . crashed my father's car."

"WHAT WERE YOU DOING DRIVING YOUR DAD'S CAR?" Rollins bellows into the phone. I have to hold it a few inches away from my ear.

"I don't know how to explain it. I fell asleep listening to your show. And then I thought I was having that dream again . . ." I swallow. "But it wasn't a dream."

"What are you saying, Vee?"

"I thought I was dreaming about riding in a car, but this time I was driving . . ." My breathing becomes labored as I find myself living through it all again. "I pulled the wheel to the right and went off the road. Right into a telephone pole. Slammed my head into the window."

"Wait. So you woke up driving your father's car?"

"Yeah."

"Do you think this is a symptom of your condition? Like sleepwalking or something? Sleepdriving?"

"It's never happened to me before," I say, pulling at the hem of my sweatshirt. "It was so strange, how I blacked out and found myself in the car. It was almost like—"

"Like what?"

I shut my eyes tight, knowing how crazy I sound.

"Like someone slid into me. Like someone forced me to get into that car."

I can almost see Rollins frowning. He only recently learned about my sliding. I suppose it's a little much to expect him to believe there are others like me out there, much less those who live in Iowa City.

"That doesn't make any sense," he says. "Don't you have to be touching a physical object that someone's imprinted on in order to slide into them? If what you're saying is true, someone in this town with the same power as you would have had to touch something of yours to force you to take your dad's car. And they'd need a motive to do such a thing. It just seems a little far-fetched to me."

"I know it doesn't make sense. It's just a feeling I had."

He rushes to say, "It's not that I don't believe you. I do. I'm just wondering if you're misinterpreting exactly what happened tonight. I know you haven't been sleeping well. Maybe you started to have that nightmare about Zane dying, but this time you acted it out. In your sleep."

I think about it. Rollins's explanation seems plausible, but I just *know* that's not what happened. Something deep down inside me keeps insisting that I was manipulated somehow tonight.

"So how did you end up getting home?"

"That's another weird thing. This woman . . . Diane, she said her name was. She happened to be driving by and she gave me a ride home. But . . ."

"But what?"

"But I don't think I gave her directions. She just seemed to know where I live."

Rollins digests this information. "Are you sure? You

did hit your head in the accident, right? Maybe you forgot about telling her."

"Maybe," I say.

After getting off the phone with Rollins, I lie in bed with my eyes wide open for a long time.

CHAPTER FIVE

The next morning, my phone buzzes with a text, waking me up. I glance at my alarm clock and realize I'm running late for school. Rollins will be here to pick me up any minute.

I peek at my phone. The text is from Rollins.

U AWAKE?

My thumbs fly over the keypad as I respond.

YEAH. BE READY IN 10.

Rollins texts back that he'll see me soon. I pull on some jeans and slide the phone into my back pocket before heading downstairs. I find my father sitting at the kitchen table, reading the newspaper.

"How are you feeling?" he asks. "Do you have whiplash? Feel like you want to see a doctor?"

I grin. "I'm seeing one right now, silly."

The anxiety in his eyes melts away, and he snorts. "Ha. But really. How does your head feel? Any dizziness? Nausea?"

Patting my father's hand reassuringly, I say, "I'm fine. Promise."

I sit down at the table, and my father pushes a glass of orange juice my way. I drink half of it in one long gulp.

"Well, I'm glad you're okay. I know you don't want to go to a doctor, but if this is a new symptom, we should really get you checked out. We can't have you sleepdriving at night. You could have been killed."

Sleepdriving. Is that even a thing?

"I seriously think it was a fluke, Dad. But if it makes you feel better, you can lock me in my room at night."

He rolls his eyes. "I might take you up on that. Now can you tell me where I might find my car?"

"It's a little off Highway 6. About five miles south of town," I say, remembering the road signs I encountered on my hike.

"Uggggggggggggggggggggggggggh." My sister shuffles into the room, looking even more disheveled than I feel this morning. She must have been having nightmares about dead girls again. "Thank God it's Friday." Mattie grabs a coffee cup and fills it to the brim. I look on with envy. Perhaps I could have just a little caffeine to get through today. I'm operating on about three hours of sleep.

But before I have a chance to act on my impulse, I hear a car pull into our driveway, the radio so loud I can hear the opening notes of a Chevelle song from where I sit.

"Rollins is here," I tell my dad. I gulp the rest of my orange juice and stand up. "Are you riding with us today?" I ask Mattie.

She nods and takes another sip of coffee before dumping the rest down the sink. Something in me dies a little as I watch the black deliciousness swirl down the drain.

"You sure you're okay, Vee?" my dad asks.

"Yeah. Totally fine. If I start to feel sick, I'll go to the nurse. Okay?"

Reluctantly, he agrees. I swoop down to give him a quick kiss and then dart out the door with Mattie following close behind.

Rollins doesn't even wait for me to fasten my seat belt before he starts in on me. "How are you this morning, Vee? Are you sure you should go to school?"

Mattie drops into the seat behind me. "Dude, why is everyone so concerned about you today?"

Rollins throws me a curious glance. "You didn't tell her?"

I shrug. "It's not a big deal."

"What's not a big deal?" Mattie asks. In the rearview mirror, I see her checking her cell phone. She's obviously very worried about my well-being.

"Oh, nothing. I just totaled Dad's car in the middle of the night."

I probably shouldn't get so much satisfaction from the shocked look my sister gives me. "What? How did that happen? Are you okay?"

Feeling sort of bad for springing my accident on Mattie, I turn around to face her. "Calm down, Matt. Look at me. I'm all in one piece." I make a split-second decision not to tell her about the whole driving-while-sleeping thing and the bizarre encounter with the woman, because she looks so alarmed already. At least, I'll stay quiet for now. "Don't worry. It's no big deal."

When I turn to face the front, Rollins gives me a questioning look. I mouth the word *later* at him and then fiddle with the radio. He growls and swats my hand away. Melting back into my seat, I welcome the normalcy of the scene. Rollins, rocking out behind the wheel. Mattie, in the back, scrutinizing a text message on her phone.

Then there's me, wondering if there was someone else in my head last night.

An impostor.

CHAPTER SIX

There's a girl waiting for Rollins at his locker. She's curvy with black, choppy hair and a tattoo that runs the full length of her right arm. As we come near, I let my gaze trace over the tattoo. It's full color and totally gorgeous, a depiction of Alice from *Alice in Wonderland* chasing the white rabbit. The girl's eyes light up when she sees Rollins.

"Aw, hey." Rollins gives the girl a hug. Jealousy prickles up my spine. He turns toward me. "Vee, this is Anna. She's been training me at the radio station."

I lift my face to hers and somehow manage a smile. The most distinctive feature of Anna's face is her eyes, which are the most startling purple color with eyelashes that seem to go on for miles. I wonder if she's wearing contacts because I've never seen eyes that color before. She's wearing a lacy baby-doll dress over rainbow-striped tights and combat boots.

She is everything that I am not.

Suddenly I start to feel sick, remembering the song

Rollins played last night. I'd kind of assumed he was thinking of me when he played it. But what if, the whole time Dave Grohl was singing, Rollins had been staring at this beautiful girl? The thought is so uncomfortable, I banish it from my mind. I am the one he loves. He told me as much that night he rescued me from the fire. True, that was six months ago, but still—could his feelings have changed that much?

"Hi, Vee," Anna says, holding out her hand to shake mine. I pump perhaps too vigorously and then feel like an idiot.

"Hello," I say. "Cool tattoo."

Can she hear the envy in my voice?

She touches her arm gently. "Thanks. The artist is a good friend of mine. If you ever want to get a tat, let me know. I can get you a special deal."

Rollins laughs. "I don't think Vee is exactly a tattoo kind of girl."

I scowl at him. "I like tattoos. Why would you think I'm not into them?" I turn to Anna. "I used to have pink hair, you know. I only recently dyed it back because . . . because I was bored with it."

I don't know why I said that. I guess it's because I feel out of place somehow. Anna and Rollins just look like they belong together with their piercings and tattoos. And then there's me . . . former preppy cheerleader turned narcoleptic slider.

Anna nods politely. "Well, Rollins, I'll catch you

tomorrow night if I don't see you before then." She disappears into the crowd.

I stuff my hands into my pockets so Rollins won't see how my fingernails are digging into my palms. "She seems nice," I say in a strained voice.

"Oh, yeah. She's really cool. Knows her music, too."

"Oh." I don't dare say anything else, in case the jealousy I'm feeling will come through in my words. How can I be feeling jealous? This is Rollins, my best friend. Of course he can have another friend. He *should* have other friends. I'm so ridiculous sometimes.

But then I wonder, as I watch him slam his locker shut and head toward first period, what if he likes her as *more* than a friend? What would I do then?

The five-minute bell rings, saving me from my thoughts. I rush to my locker and grab my books for English class. As I reach into my backpack to grab a pen, my fingers brush against an old bottle of caffeine pills I stashed away for emergencies. I let my hand linger for just a moment and then pull it away.

My head throbs from lack of sleep. As Mrs. Winger works her way up and down the aisles, picking up homework, I feel my eyes droop.

"Look alive, Sylvia," Mrs. Winger says, stopping at my desk. "Do you have the assignment?"

I open my folder and pretend to look through the papers, even though I know I didn't do the work. I'd planned to do my homework while I listened to Rollins's show, but I ended up falling asleep instead. Perhaps I could bring up the car accident for sympathy points. But, no, then everyone would just think I'm weirder than they already do. Add sleepdriving to my narcolepsy and I'm a Grade-A Freak.

"Sorry, Mrs. Winger. I must have left it at home."

She shakes her head as though she doesn't believe me and moves on to Samantha, who looks even worse than I feel. Her hair, usually perfectly straightened, is swept back in a messy ponytail. She's not wearing any makeup, and there are huge circles beneath her eyes. Remembering how she was drunkenly singing in the back of Scotch's car, I wonder just how hungover she is today. But Sam doesn't just look dehydrated. She looks regretful or something. Her demeanor unsettles me, reminds me of how I felt the morning after the homecoming dance last year. I wonder if something happened to her. I wouldn't put it past Scotch to take advantage of an inebriated girl. If Rollins hadn't burst in on us in the locker room, who knows what would have happened?

"How about you, Samantha? Did you finish the assignment?" Mrs. Winger hovers over Samantha, tapping her foot.

Samantha doesn't even pretend to look through her things. She just glares at Mrs. Winger wordlessly until the teacher gets uncomfortable and moves on. Sam must sense my eyes on her because she then levels her gaze at me. I don't look away.

She continues to give me her patented death stare while

I scoot into the empty desk between us so I can talk to her without Mrs. Winger, who has moved to the back of the room, hearing our conversation.

"Hey, Sam," I say, using her nickname for the first time in ages. It feels strange on my tongue. "Everything okay?"

Samantha crosses her arms over her chest. "What do you care?"

I hesitate. Samantha was so out of it last night. Unless Scotch told her about our encounter, which I'm thinking is highly unlikely, she probably has no idea that I saw her in Scotch's car. If I explain, I'll have to tell her about the car crash, which I really don't want people finding out about. But if I don't tell her, I'll just look really nosy.

In the end, I choose nosiness over freakishness.

"Did you have a rough night?" I ask, hoping to sound sympathetic.

She narrows her eyes. "Why? What did you hear?"

I try to look innocent. "Nothing. You look kind of tired this morning, that's all. Just wanted to make sure you're all right."

My neighborly concern doesn't seem to be winning Samantha over. She pulls out a notebook, flips to a clean page, and writes the date at the top. I realize that she's ignoring me.

"Samantha, we don't have to be enemies," I say, thinking how false the words sound even as they come out of my mouth. Nothing has changed since I tried to save her life. I am still the girl who went out with the guy she had a crush on. She is still the girl who told everyone I was a slut. She is still the girl who watched Scotch drag me into the boys' locker room and didn't do a thing to help me. A few words aren't going to change that. Still, I want to try. "I don't hate you."

Samantha makes a disgusted noise and sets down her pen deliberately. "Vee, I don't give a shit if you hate me or not. You are, like, the least of my concerns this morning."

Her outburst wasn't exactly what I was going for, but it's something. At least she's admitting that there's *something* going on with her.

"What *is* your biggest concern this morning?"

The look Samantha gives me could freeze Satan himself. "None of your effing business." She picks up her pen again, and I know I've been defeated.

Mrs. Winger moves to the front of the classroom and starts to talk about the Puritans. Reluctantly, I return to my seat. The rest of the period crawls by. I keep sneaking peeks at Samantha, but she is either really immersed in Mrs. Winger's lecture or completely determined to pay no attention to me whatsoever. At the end of the period, she stuffs her notebook and pen into her oversized purse and rockets out of the room, never once looking my way.

I sit in the back of the library with the tattered copy of *Sports Illustrated* lying open before me. Before I try to slide, I wait for the librarian to take attendance and then sit down with her own magazine.

I've gotten to the point where I'm almost always successful at triggering slides, except when I'm amped up on caffeine. Thank God I didn't give in to the pills in my bag this morning. Otherwise I don't think this would work.

I'm going to slide into Scotch and see if I can figure out exactly what went down last night. He'll be in gym class. If I'm lucky, he'll be gossiping with his jock friend again. If something did happen with Samantha, I'm sure he'll be bragging about it to the whole school.

Once the librarian settles down with her copy of Crock-Pot Adventures or whatever the hell she's reading, I run my fingers over the glossy pages of the magazine. I've opened it to an article about some NFL player who overcame great adversity—family problems, health problems, academic problems—to get where he is today. The page has been turned down, as if someone wanted to return to it for inspiration. I wonder if that person was Scotch.

I rest my head on my desk as the bookshelves of the library melt away, turning into basketball hoops and banners in our school's colors. Just like the last time I slid into Scotch, the students are doing laps.

Scotch's sneakered feet slap against the wooden floor. His breathing is more labored than it was the last time I was inside him. He's probably feeling the ill effects of the alcohol from last night's party. Serves him right.

"So how was it?" a voice to my right asks.

Randall Fritz.

Here comes the part where Scotch brags about his conquest to his friend. I brace myself for a detailed description of Scotch's sexual prowess. And then a troubling thought occurs to me. There's no way for me to verify whether Scotch is telling the truth. If he says he had sex with Samantha, it could be true or it could be a lie. If it is true, having sex with a practically unconscious girl makes Scotch a date rapist. If it's a lie, that just makes him scum.

Before I can think about what I'll do if Scotch *does* say he hooked up with Samantha, he throws a curveball.

"Oh, man. Last night was so freaky. So Samantha and I were driving out in the country, looking for a quiet place to have some privacy if you know what I mean . . . and who do you think we came across, just walking along the side of the road?"

Oh shit. Hold everything.

"Who?" Randall asks, panting for some juicy gossip.

"Vee Bell."

"Damn," Randall says. "She is *hot*. Especially since she dyed her hair back and doesn't look like such a freak anymore. Tell me, did you get some of that?"

Scotch stops running for a second. "Do you even need to ask? Vee's had the hots for me since freshman year. I went out with her last year, but then I had to cut her off when she went through that weird goth phase. But she was begging for it last night."

Scotch stops speaking and starts grinding his teeth together. Without my realizing it, the rage brewing inside me has taken over. "Asshole," I mutter.

Randall looks confused. "Uh, did you just call me an asshole?"

"Misogynistic douche bag." I can't help it. The words just fly out of Scotch's mouth.

"Wait. Miss-oh-ginous . . . what?" Randall scratches his head.

"You want to know what really happened last night?" I ask. Since we've stopped running, more and more people are slowing down to listen to our conversation. The gym teacher has disappeared into his office.

Randall looks seriously freaked out now. "Um. Okay?"

I take a deep breath. "Last night, I dropped Samantha off so I could go home and watch some *Golden Girls*. That Betty White gets me hot, *if you know what I mean*." I wink at Randall twice, and he turns bright red.

A couple of girls start to laugh.

"What did he just say?" asks a guy with a fauxhawk.

"I think he just said he whacks it to *Golden Girls*," a girl in a pink Juicy Couture sweatshirt answers helpfully.

Considering my job done, I slide back into my own body. I lift my head from the desk and realize I've drooled a little bit on the copy of *Sports Illustrated*. I wipe the corner of my mouth with my sleeve. The librarian didn't even notice me appear to fall asleep.

CHAPTER SEVEN

After school, Rollins waits for me in his car. He's got his radio turned up and is beating his hands on the steering wheel, but the minute I open the passenger door, he shuts off the music.

"So I heard an interesting rumor today," he says, crossing his arms. "I thought you might know a little something about it."

"Oh yeah?" I ask innocently, arranging my backpack on the floor.

"Evidently Scotch Becker announced his fondness for Betty White today in gym class?"

I'm unable to suppress a smirk. The rumor had spread like wildfire, and almost everyone was talking about it by lunchtime. I overheard Scotch in the hallway, bewildered, trying to explain to his football buddies that it was all a joke. I almost felt sorry for him. Almost.

"Not that I'm Scotch's biggest fan, but why would you do that to him?" Rollins asks, sounding genuinely flabbergasted. "Yeah, the guy's an ass, but you don't need to be messing with his head."

It occurs to me that, in the confusion of last night, I never did tell Rollins about running into Scotch or how Samantha was wasted in the back of his car. Quickly, I fill him in, explaining how distraught Samantha seemed in English this morning and how I slid into Scotch to find out what really happened between the two of them. When I get to the part about Scotch claiming that *I* came onto *him* last night, Rollins holds up his hand for me to stop. He looks like he's going to puke.

"Okay, okay, I get the picture. I guess it served him right. Do you really think he took advantage of Samantha?"

I shrug. "There's no way to know. Scotch is a lying sack of shit, and Sam doesn't trust me enough to tell the truth. I hope he's all talk. For her sake."

Rollins shakes his head. "If I ever hear him talking about you that way . . ."

"Hey," I say softly, reaching out to grab his arm. "I can take care of myself."

Rollins stares at me for a moment and then nods, starting the car.

"So. Friday Night Fright?" I ask, mentally thumbing through my DVDs, wondering which horror flick we should watch.

"Uh, yeah. I have some things to do first, though," Rollins says vaguely.

"Oh," I say. "Okay."

It's not unusual for Rollins to have to run home and give his mother supper and get her ready for bed before he comes over, but he's usually pretty up-front about it—at least, he has been since I learned about his mother's condition. However, something about the way he's avoiding my gaze makes me feel like he's trying to hide something.

We don't say anything more until he pulls into my driveway. I grab my backpack, trying to think of something lighthearted to say to ease the awkwardness between us. "I, um, guess I'll see you later."

"Later." He barely waits for me to close the door before he's backing out into the street—a definite contrast to the way he usually waits for me to get inside before he leaves. As I watch him disappear around the corner, I feel a bit queasy. If he's not going home, where is he going?

Some part of me wonders if, wherever he's going, Anna will be there.

Onscreen, Jason Voorhees chases some poor girl through the woods. Mattie and her friend Regina are sprawled on the floor, devouring a bowl of popcorn.

Mattie started hanging out with Regina a lot after Sophie and Amber died. She's a sweet girl, but she kind of reminds me of Eeyore. Her older brother, Todd, was killed in a boating accident a few years ago, and she brings him up all the time. One minute she'll be talking about how hot the new band teacher is, and the next she'll be in tears because she remembers how her brother used to play the clarinet in elementary school. It's exhausting to spend time with her, but I think she gets Mattie in a way that few other people do.

Rollins sits inches away from me on the couch. Almost everything about him is familiar—the scent of leather that lingers on him long after he takes off his jacket, the way his lip ring shines in the light from the television, the warmth that emanates off his body in our otherwise chilly living room.

But there's something about him that's changed. There's a tension in his shoulders, as if he isn't completely comfortable sitting this close to me. I wonder if it's because he's thinking about Anna.

God, these thoughts are torturous. And I feel ridiculous, getting so worked up over practically nothing. So he has a new, hot friend. So he might have gone to see her tonight before he came over here. Why is it any of my business? Why did it take Rollins possibly being interested in someone else before I came to my senses and realized what a freaking amazing guy he is?

A loud noise causes Mattie and Regina to shriek. In the movie, Jason has jumped out at the girl, his knife blade flashing. I take the opportunity to pretend to be startled and move a bit closer to Rollins, setting my hand next to his until our pinkies meet. Almost imperceptibly, he moves an inch away from me, so we're not touching. Did he mean to do that? Can't he stand to be close to me anymore?

I look around the room, searching for some way to get Mattie and Regina to leave us alone. My eyes fall on the popcorn bowl on the floor, nearly empty. I grab the remote control and hit the Pause button.

"Hey, Mattie. Way to eat all the popcorn. Rollins and I didn't get any."

Mattie glances at the bowl and then looks up guiltily. "Oops. Sorry."

"Maybe you and Regina could go make some more?" I raise my eyebrows and tilt my head slightly toward the kitchen, hoping to convey that this is an order, not a request.

Mattie looks at me and then Rollins, and she smiles. "Oh, sure. Come on, Regina." Mattie scoops up the popcorn bowl.

"Hey, do you have any of that flavored powder to sprinkle on top?" Regina asks, following Mattie. "Todd used to love that stuff. He could go through a whole bottle in two days."

With the two gone, I turn toward Rollins. "I was hoping we'd get a moment alone to talk," I say, my heart banging so hard I'm afraid he might hear it.

I know what I have to do now. Somehow, I have to find the words to tell Rollins how I feel, before this thing with Anna gets going. Otherwise, I might lose him forever.

Rollins looks down at his hands. "About what?"

"About us," I say, my voice small.

Finally, he looks up. "What do you mean?"

Jesus, this is hard. So hard that I'm tempted to just let it go, leave things the way they are. I mean, we're best friends. Do I really want to mess that up? What if I confess my feelings for him, and Rollins denies them? What if we never speak again?

After a long moment of racking my brain for the perfect

turn of phrase, I decide maybe words are overrated. I squeeze my eyes shut tight and lean forward, my lips in a loose pout.

Nothing happens.

I open one eye. Rollins is staring at me like I've grown another head.

"What are you doing, Vee?"

Heat rushes into my cheeks. I pull back and try to act nonchalant. "Nothing. It's nothing. Don't worry about it."

His eyebrows knit together in concern. "Are you sure?"

"Yeah. I just—I don't know what I was thinking."

A buzzing noise interrupts the moment.

Rollins pulls his cell out of his pocket. It's clear that someone has called him, but he turns away slightly so I can't see who's on the other line. After a moment, he stuffs the phone back into his pocket.

"You know," he says, rising. "It's late. I should go."

"Sure," I say, standing to walk him to the door. "No problem."

"Hey, you don't need to get up. Sit down. Enjoy the movie."

"Oh, yeah."

Rollins grabs his jacket from the back of the couch and pulls it on. "I'll call you later."

"Okay," I say, mumbling. I hope it's dark enough that he can't see the tears welling up in my eyes. I'd like to think, if he did see them, he would stop. But he doesn't.

A few seconds later, I hear the door open and close.

———

I've locked myself in the downstairs bathroom while Mattie and Regina finish watching the movie. Pathetic. Here I am, weeping on the toilet like some stupid girl who's just had her heart broken. And the worst part is I should know better by now. Things like relationships just don't go well for me. I should just accept it and move on. And become a nun or something.

The thought of me in a habit, dancing around a mountaintop and singing or some crap, makes me smile. I hold on to the image as I blow my nose.

The doorbell rings.

He's back.

He's changed his mind and has come back.

I peek in the bathroom mirror and make sure my face isn't too blotchy. Then I hurry out into the foyer. The light is on outside, but through the sheer curtain, I can barely make out the figure standing there.

I throw the door open, ready to tell Rollins what an idiot I was being and that we should just stay best friends and that's totally cool with me.

But it's not Rollins standing on my front porch.

It's my dead mother.

CHAPTER EIGHT

I don't say anything. I *can't* say anything. I feel my jaw drop open, but I can't force my lips to move or exhale the breath required to make a sound.

Logically, I know this can't be my mother. I was there the day she died. I attended her funeral, dropped a single white rose onto her coffin as it was lowered into the ground. It's as though my eyes are betraying me. She's just as I remember her—long blond hair, now wet from the rain that started up soon after Rollins took off. Her eyes are bright blue, just like mine. Only her clothes are different. Instead of the ripped jeans and band T-shirts my mother wore when I was little, this woman is wearing khakis and a button-down blouse under a peacoat. She is completely soaked. Mascara trails down her cheeks, but I can't tell if it's from the weather or if she's been crying.

After a moment, I realize this must be my mother's sister, Lydia. She's the aunt I never met. My father explained she moved to California a long while ago and lost touch with the family.

"You must be Sylvia," the woman says. "You look just like your mother."

I clear my throat. "So do you."

"Who's here?" My father's voice emerges behind me.

"Hello, Jared," Lydia says, almost businesslike. "It's been a long time."

I turn to examine my father's face. He looks like he's in shock, just as I was a moment ago. He's probably struggling with the very same emotions that flooded me—longing for his wife, who passed away years ago, confusion that someone who looks so much like her could just show up on our doorstep, unannounced. He opens his mouth and then closes it again, like he's not sure what to say. I reach out and touch his arm.

"I'm sorry to just show up like this." The woman gestures to the yellow Toyota parked in the driveway. "I can leave if you like."

"No," my father says quickly. "No, don't go. I'm sorry. I just . . . wasn't prepared. Come on in. It's raining buckets outside. Don't you have an umbrella?"

I notice a small suitcase on the porch beside Lydia. She stoops down to grab the handle and then walks through the door that my father is holding open for her. I take a step back. It's so strange to see my aunt here, in my house. She honestly looks like my mother's ghost.

"I didn't bring an umbrella," Lydia explains, pulling off her soggy coat. "It was kind of a spur-of-the-moment-type thing."

My father takes the coat from her and hangs it on the

coat-tree. "You must be freezing. Would you like some coffee?"

Shivering, Lydia nods. "That would be great."

I hear a thump come from the living room, followed by giggling. If Mattie were to walk into the room right this second, I realize, she would be in for a shock.

"I'm going to go let my sister know that you're here," I say.

"Sure." Lydia gives me a knowing look, as if she understands that I might need to prepare my sister so she isn't alarmed by the Mom clone standing in our front entryway. She follows my father into the kitchen.

I spin around and head into the living room to find the movie on pause and Mattie and Regina practicing herkie jumps.

"Come on, Vee, you know how to do this one," Mattie calls out.

Ignoring her invitation, I throw her a serious look. "I need to talk to you. Right. Now."

Regina apparently catches the grave tone of my voice because she mutters something about promising her mother she'd be home for dinner, grabs her jacket, and heads for the door.

"What's up?" Mattie asks. "Does this have to do with Rollins?"

I wince, remembering the awkward way Rollins rushed out the door, but then I push the memory aside. I have bigger things to worry about right now. Like why my aunt suddenly decided to show up after all this time. Something must have happened in California, and I'm dying to know what.

"No." I grab her arm and pull her onto the couch. "Do you remember Mom talking about her older sister? The one who ran off when she was in high school?"

Mattie frowns. "Um, kind of. Wasn't her name Olivia?"

"Lydia," I correct her. "And she's in the kitchen right now, drinking coffee with Dad."

Mattie's face lights up. "Are you kidding me? Our long-lost aunt is in our house right now? Awesome!"

She jumps up, ready to run into the kitchen. I grab her hand.

"There's something else you need to know."

Mattie waits impatiently for me to go on.

"She looks a *lot* like Mom."

Shrugging, Mattie says, "Well, duh. They were sisters." She breaks free from my grasp and bolts out of the room.

I sigh, getting up to follow her. She can't say I didn't warn her.

When I reach the kitchen, I almost run into Mattie, who is frozen in the doorway. Sure enough, she is stunned by Lydia's appearance.

Lydia and my father are seated at the table, each with a coffee cup in their hands. The scene really is disorienting. It's as if my mother took a break from her afterlife to stop by and have a cup of joe with my father.

Lydia sets her coffee cup down and rises. "Matilda? My God. You're so grown-up. So beautiful."

My sister's eyes well up with tears, and I wonder how

long she's been waiting for someone to say those exact words. How fitting for her to hear them from a woman who could be my mother's doppelgänger.

Mattie releases a shuddering sob and then rushes into Lydia's arms. I watch them for a moment, and then look at my father, wondering what he makes of all this. His face is twisted into a little frown.

It is decided that Lydia will stay in Mattie's room for the evening, and Mattie will sleep in my room. After my father gives Lydia a little tour, he hands her a couple of towels and leaves her in the bathroom to get washed up.

My father, Mattie, and I sit around the kitchen table. Mattie has a million questions about Lydia. I keep my mouth shut and listen.

"Why has she been in California all this time? Why did she never come to see us?"

My father rubs his temples wearily. "She and your mother had a huge fight over a boy back when they were in high school. Lydia accused your mom of stealing her boyfriend. She took a CD that your mom had saved up for, U2's *The Joshua Tree*, I think it was. . . ." Dad pauses to smile faintly. "And broke it into tiny pieces over your mother's bed."

I bite my thumbnail. "Is that it? She broke one of Mom's CDs?"

"It was her favorite CD," my father says. "And you know how your mother felt about her music. Plus, Lydia said some really terrible things, like how she'd destroy everything your mother ever loved. Shortly after, she ran away, and she took your mother's college fund with her. As far as I know, that's the last time the two ever saw each other."

"Should we be letting her stay with us if she's so terrible?" I ask.

My father shrugs. "She's family. Where else would she stay? Besides, that was all a long time ago. People do change, honey."

I look away. There's an undercurrent in his words, almost as if he is referring to himself. After all, we recently found out that my father had an affair when my mother was dying of cancer. He had a baby out of wedlock and never told us. Only in the past couple of months have I really started to trust him again.

Mattie pokes me in the side. "Lighten up, Vee. It's going to be fun, having her stay with us. She'll have so many stories to tell us about Mom when she was a kid. Don't you think, Dad?"

My dad forces his lips into a smile. "I'm sure she will."

I don't blame Mattie for her enthusiasm. She's always complained that she doesn't have any memories of our mother. Maybe Mattie is right. Lydia might be able to tell us things about our mother that my father never could. I've always wondered if she could slide. Maybe Lydia can confirm my suspicions.

"How long is she going to stay with us?" I look at my father.

"A few weeks."

"Did you ask her why she came back *now*? I mean, it's been more than twenty years. Why didn't she come back when you guys got married? Or when me and Mattie were born? Or at least when Mom *died*?"

He sighs. "I suspect that she's feeling very guilty for missing out on all that, Vee. Maybe she wasn't ready yet."

This answer doesn't fully satisfy me. There has to be more to her sudden appearance. Why is she here *now*?

As Mattie and I walk down the hall to my bedroom, the bathroom door opens. Steam escapes from within, and Lydia appears, toweling her hair dry. My father loaned her his bathrobe to wear. It's huge on her, but she doesn't seem to mind. It makes me feel strange, seeing her wrapped up in his clothes. I remember my mother stealing that same robe, claiming that it was so much roomier and more comfortable than her own.

"Girls, I want to thank you so much for letting me stay. I know it must be strange. After all, this is the first time we've met. But I just know we're going to be great friends, the three of us." She flashes a bright smile.

Mattie doesn't miss a beat. "My catsa sue catsa. Or something. I'm not all that great at Spanish."

Lydia laughs. "That wasn't my favorite class, either."

"Do you need anything?" I ask. "Toothbrush? Another pillow?"

She holds up a pink toothbrush. "I'm covered."

"Well, good night then." I open my bedroom door.

"Sweet dreams," Lydia says, reaching out and ruffling Mattie's hair. Something about the gesture irks me, but I can't articulate what it is. Mattie just smiles and follows me into my room.

After I close my door behind us, Mattie sighs happily. "This is going to be great."

I nod, but inside I'm not sure I agree.

CHAPTER NINE

As Mattie strips off her jeans and pink top and shim-mies into her pajamas, I run a brush through my hair. My weariness comes on all at once. First the thing with Rollins, and then an aunt who I've never met before showing up on our doorstep. Yawning, I change into an oversized Radiohead T-shirt.

Mattie slips under the covers, her cheeks glowing. "Isn't she beautiful?" she asks as I lie down next to her.

I punch my pillow. "Yeah. She looks just like Mom."

Mattie is quiet then for a moment, just staring up at the ceiling. It's been a long time since I've seen her like this. Peaceful. Hopeful, even. Finally, she flips over and props her chin up with the palm of her hand. "Can I tell you a secret?"

Even though I want badly to just turn over and go to sleep, I force a smile. "Sure. What's up?"

"There's this guy . . ." Mattie says softly, her eyes bright.

"Yeah . . . ?" I prompt, my faux smile turning genuine. In this moment, she reminds me so much of the old Mattie, the outgoing one with a million friends and a different crush every week.

Her face reddens slightly. "Russ White."

I cover my mouth, trying to hide my amusement. "Really." Russ White is a tall, good-looking senior with glasses. The reason I'm so surprised is that he's not Mattie's type. He's not popular in the usual way—he's not athletic or party-obsessed. He's actually my age, but he's so smart he skipped a grade in elementary school. Known for being kind to everyone, he has an infectious smile and a great sense of humor. Everyone likes him, but I've never known him to have a girlfriend.

My sister rolls onto her back. "Of course. He's hot."

I cock my head to the side. It's true. He is hot, in a studious sort of way.

Mattie kicks one of her legs up in the air and examines her pedicure. She starts to ramble, explaining the story of how she met Russ.

"I was in the library trying to check out a book for my history project, but Mrs. Nelson was saying I owed a fine for some vampire book I checked out at the beginning of the year. I told her I paid it already, but she wouldn't believe me. Russ must have overheard us because he came over and paid Mrs. Nelson. After I checked out the book, he introduced himself to me. And he asked me to go to a movie with him! Do you think Dad will let me go? I know he's a senior, but . . ."

"Yeah, he's a senior, but he's my age. It's not that

weird. You guys are only two years apart. How about this? Rollins and I will go with you. Maybe we can see the new *Scar* film." The words are out of my mouth before I remember the weirdness between Rollins and me. Will the embarrassment of tonight fade before next weekend? I hope so.

Mattie throws her arms around me. "Really? That would be great." After a beat, she pulls away and rolls over, facing the wall. "Night," she says.

"Night," I tell her, reaching to turn out the lamp on my bedside table. As I drift off, I think to myself how nice it is that Mattie's able to confide in me about these sorts of things. Six months ago, we never talked like this. I feel a kinship with her that I've never felt before. I wonder if, sometime soon, I might be able to tell her *my* biggest secret.

A loud clattering wakes me.

The noise is coming from downstairs.

Mattie is still fast asleep, so I gently push back the covers and swing my feet onto the floor. The carpet mutes my footsteps as I cross the room. In the hallway, I see that the door to Mattie's room is closed, but my father's door is standing wide open. I peek inside, but the bed is empty.

Another crash startles me.

It seems to be coming from the living room.

I tiptoe down the stairs.

My hands are shaking, my heart ricocheting off my rib cage. What if there's an intruder? What if my father is fighting with him? I look around for some sort of weapon, but there's nothing.

When I reach the landing, I peek around the corner. My father stands with his back to me. He seems to be going through the pictures on the bookshelf, grabbing one after another and throwing them to the floor. There's a pile of broken glass at his feet.

He grabs a wedding portrait and flings it down. Jagged pieces bounce off the carpet and land near my feet.

"Dad?"

He freezes. Turns slowly in my direction.

"Dad? What are you doing?"

He takes a few dazed steps toward me. The look in his eyes is strange, as if he's not aware of his actions, as if he's not even there. It reminds me of that day in English class, when I seemed to lose control of my body. It was like I was there, but not really. Like someone else had taken my place.

"Dad?"

The cloudy expression clears, and he shakes his head. He makes eye contact with me and seems to recognize my face. "Vee? What the hell? What's going on?" Bewildered, he looks at the mess on the floor.

"Um. You were throwing pictures on the floor. Don't you remember?"

I can tell from the look on his face that he doesn't. At all. Suddenly I think I might know who's behind his strange behavior and my car accident.

Someone is sliding into us.

Someone who just happened to show up for the first time in years.

"Everything okay in here?"

I turn to find Aunt Lydia standing in the doorway, tying the sash on my father's robe, concern etched into her features.

CHAPTER TEN

On Monday morning, Rollins shows up to give Mattie and me a ride to school, just like normal. What isn't normal is the silence in the car. Rollins doesn't even have the radio on. Mattie, who's exhausted from tossing and turning all night, rests her head against the window with her eyes closed. The only sound is me flipping through the pages of my math notebook, pretending to study for a nonexistent quiz.

I peek at Rollins every once in a while. His shoulders seem tense, and his face is like a mask. I wonder what he's thinking about, if—like me—his mind is set on that terrible moment when I closed my eyes and pouted my lips . . . and he just stared at me.

Thinking of the moment again makes me shrink into myself. I look out the window for the rest of the car ride, counting down the seconds until we get to school and I can get away from Rollins.

"Thanks for the ride," I say too loudly when the car comes to a stop in the school parking lot. Rollins opens his mouth like he's going to respond, but I'm too quick and shut the door before he can say anything.

"Whoa Nelly," Mattie says, hurrying to keep up with me. "What was that back there?"

"What was what?" I toss back at her. She pulls on my sleeve, forcing me to stop.

"You know what. Deathly silence. Something happened between you and Rollins, didn't it?" Mattie crosses her arms over her chest.

"I thought you were sleeping," I say, shoving my notebook into my backpack.

Mattie's voice turns stern. "Sylvia Bell, you tell me the truth right this instant. Why are you and Rollins acting so weird?"

Fairly sure I'm not going to get out of this interrogation without telling Mattie exactly what happened, I sigh. Before I say anything, though, I look around to make sure no one is within earshot. "If you must know, I gave Rollins every opportunity to kiss me on Friday night."

Mattie squeals. "Really? Vee, that's great!"

I glare at her. "You know what's not so great? He just stared at me like I was stupid or something. It was the most awkward moment of my entire life."

Mattie shocks me by laughing.

I spin on my heel and walk toward the school's entrance, furious. I should have known better than to tell Mattie. There's no way she can understand the implications of what happened between Rollins and me. Our friendship is basically ruined. There's no going back to just being friends.

That moment will always be hanging there between us.

Mattie catches the back of my shirt. "Slow down. I'm sorry for laughing. It's just that you probably stunned the poor guy. He's been pining after you for months, and all of a sudden you throw yourself at him? No wonder he's confused."

I shake off her hand. "I didn't *throw* myself at him."

"Come on. Admit it. You've been giving him mixed signals ever since Zane died. At first you were all like, 'Woe is me. I've been betrayed. I'll never love again.' And now you want to make out with Rollins? It's a little bit sudden, is all I'm saying."

I cock my head. She does have a point. I've been pushing Rollins away for so long now. It must seem strange for me to change my tune so quickly. Maybe I'm being a little too dramatic. I should give him another chance.

"Listen to your genius little sister. Rollins worships the ground you walk on. I'm sure that didn't change overnight," Mattie says teasingly. "Just talk to him at lunch. And don't forget to ask him about seeing *Scar* with me and Russ this weekend."

"All right, all right," I mutter. "I'll see what I can do."

"Atta girl." Mattie slaps me on the back.

At first, I'm not even sure Rollins is going to show up at our meeting place under the bleachers at lunch. Five minutes pass, then ten, then fifteen. Finally, I hear the familiar crunch of leaves as he makes his way toward me. Taking a big bite of my brown-sugar cinnamon Pop-Tart,

I nonchalantly stare out at the empty football field, like I haven't been counting the minutes until he showed up.

"Hey," he says, plopping down next to me.

"Hey," I say, and then take another bite.

I notice Rollins is sitting a little farther away from me than usual. He doesn't meet my eyes. Instead, he pulls out a Sharpie and focuses on the intricate design he's been doodling on the bottom of his shoes for the past few weeks.

"Sorry I'm late," he says. "I was talking to Anna. It sounds like she can get me an interview with Who Killed My Sea Monkeys for my zine."

"Awesome," I say, hoping my enthusiasm doesn't sound too fake. Rollins writes, designs, and produces his own magazine, which he passes around school and hands to strangers on buses. Though he editorializes about stuff that happens at school and world events in general, his focus is definitely on music.

"Yeah," he agrees. "I'm pretty stoked."

Silence.

I take another bite of Pop-Tart. It tastes like sand.

"So . . . anything new with you?" Rollins asks, his voice strained. He's clearly trying to move past this weirdness between us.

I search for something to talk about. Then I realize I haven't even told Rollins about my aunt Lydia randomly showing up on our doorstep. Under normal circumstances, Rollins would have been the first person I called.

"Yeah, actually," I say. "You'll never guess who showed up Friday night after—after you left."

Rollins looks uncomfortable at the reference to his abrupt departure. "Who?"

"My aunt Lydia, who I've never met before. I guess she ran away to California when she was a teenager and never came back. Until now. Anyway, she turned up on our doorstep with a suitcase."

"Crazy," Rollins says. "What does she want?"

"She claims she just wants to get to know her family, but I think that's just a cover story. She could have come back at any time, right? Besides, some really weird stuff has been happening since she got here."

Rollins twirls his Sharpie, looking interested. I'm relieved that Lydia's sudden appearance has given us something neutral to talk about. "What weird stuff?"

"Well, think about it. I got into that accident on Thursday night. What if she had something to do with it? She could have gotten here on Thursday and stayed at a hotel or something. Maybe she's able to slide. Maybe she forced me to steal my dad's car and drive out into the country."

Rollins looks doubtful. "But *why*? What would be her motivation?"

"That's the kicker. My dad said she got into a huge fight with my mom when they were in high school. She vowed to destroy everything my mom ever loved. Hence the car accident. She's trying to kill me."

Rollins clears his throat. "If she actually slid into you, wouldn't she need something with your emotional imprint on it? She would've needed it before she even got to your house, since someone slid into you the night before, right?"

Stupid, rational Rollins.

"Well, what about this? Last night I woke up to a crashing noise. When I went downstairs, I found my dad throwing pictures everywhere. He busted his own wedding portrait. He was totally out of it, like someone else was controlling his actions. When he finally realized where he was, Lydia showed up. And *she was wearing his bathrobe*."

The dubious expression on Rollins's face gives way to thoughtfulness. "That is a pretty big coincidence."

"Right? If she slid into him, she was forcing him to break wedding pictures of his dead wife. Pretty sick."

"I don't know. It still seems like a stretch. Saying you'll destroy everything someone loves is pretty melodramatic, like something you'd say during a fight and then forget five minutes later. I seriously doubt she's trying to wreck your family. I bet Lydia just realized how lonely she was and decided to come back and meet her nieces."

I crumple up the wrapper from my Pop-Tart. "Maybe . . ." I say, even though I don't really believe it. "Oh, hey. I'm supposed to ask if you'll go with me and Mattie and Russ White to *Scar* this weekend."

Rollins goes back to doodling on his shoe. "Russ White?"

"Yeah, you know the senior who should be in our grade but skipped a year in elementary?" Rollins's face is blank, and I remind myself that he wasn't here in elementary school. "He's the guy who drives the silver pickup you're always drooling over." Rollins nods in recognition.

"Apparently he's the white knight of library fines," I joke, and go on to explain the story of how Russ introduced himself to Mattie. Rollins chuckles.

"So would you be willing to play chaperone with me on Saturday? I know you wanted to see *Scar*, so we can kill two birds with one stone."

Rollins sighs. "I guess so, but I'm not going to lie—I'm not all that psyched about spending another Saturday night babysitting your sister."

"We won't have to babysit her," I say, slightly irritated. "We can sit in the back and whisper snarky things during the stupid parts, like always. I just need to be in the general vicinity."

Rollins must sense my annoyance because he reaches over and grabs my shoulder. "Hey, of course I'm in. Friends?"

I take a deep breath. This is what I want, isn't it?

"Friends."

CHAPTER ELEVEN

Instead of heading to my afternoon gym class, I duck into the computer lab. I'm not too worried about getting into trouble. The teacher forgets to take attendance half of the time, and even if he does mark me as absent, I can make something up about having a narcoleptic episode.

There are only a few kids in the lab. One appears to be watching music videos on YouTube. He has headphones on and doesn't notice me drop into the chair next to him.

My curiosity about Aunt Lydia has gotten the best of me. Maybe Rollins is right and she is just a lonely woman seeking out the family she left behind so long ago, but I can't help wondering if there was some sort of impetus that brought her to us.

The school's home page pops up, and I highlight the URL and type in Google. In the search field, I type in "Lydia Homer." Homer was my mother's maiden name. Since Lydia isn't married (that I know of), I'm guessing that's the name she went by in California. Millions of results pop up. I sift through them, not finding anything especially helpful. There's a woman living in Missouri by that name, but when I click on her Facebook page, the picture doesn't look anything like Lydia. Another woman in Idaho. I go back up to the top of the page and narrow my results to California. This leads me to the website of a dog trainer living in San Francisco, but again, the picture looks nothing like my aunt.

Twenty minutes go by, and I find nothing about my aunt. It seems odd that someone could live in today's world without leaving any tracks on Google. I drum my fingers on the desk in frustration. Finally, the bell rings, and I log off the computer, thinking about how much I'd suck as a private investigator.

After school, I'm standing at my locker, contemplating which books I need to take home with me. Samantha Phillips stands nearby, gazing at herself in her locker mirror with a tube of lip gloss in her hand.

A few feet away, a couple of sophomore football players are huddled together. They keep looking over at Samantha and laughing. When she notices them, she slams her locker shut and strides across the hall to face them. "What the hell are you laughing at?"

I expect the sophomores to cower before her, but one of them looks her right in the eye and says, "Did you have a good time with Scotch on Thursday night? Because I heard you did. In fact, I saw evidence that you had a *really* good time." The guy's friend cracks up.

Samantha turns white. She backs away from the guys, who are now slapping each other on the back and roaring with laughter. Then she turns and runs down the hallway before ducking into the girls' bathroom.

A debate rages within me. If Samantha and I were still best friends, I would immediately chase after her and make sure she was okay. Now we have this chasm between us. But I have to admit there's a part of me that still cares about her. Plus, I'm curious about the evidence the guy was alluding to. Finally, I decide to go after her, even though she'll probably brush me off like she did last week.

I take a deep breath and fight my way down the hall, through the crowd of students all anxious to get to their after-school activities or to just go home. I push the bathroom door open.

I hear the unmistakable sound of Samantha sobbing in one of the stalls. She gasps and stops crying, though, as soon as I walk in. Same old Samantha. She could never let anyone see her wounded.

"Samantha? It's me, Vee."

I hear her blow her nose, and then the toilet flushes.

"Sam? You okay?"

She opens the door and steps into the harsh fluorescent light, straightening her skirt. Her eyes are dry, but her cheeks are all splotchy and red. She takes a few steps to the nearest sink and starts to wash her hands.

"What do you want?" she asks, looking at me in the mirror.

"I—I saw you run in here, and I thought you were upset."

After drying her hands, she turns around and leans against the sink. "Why would *you* care? Of all people, why you?" The question cuts me to the bone. Sure, we haven't been friendly in a while, but that doesn't mean she doesn't matter to me, even after the terrible rumors she spread when I went out with Scotch.

"Why wouldn't I care?" I ask gently.

"Um, because I've been a major bitch to you this last year? If I were you, I wouldn't even speak to me." Samantha's voice breaks, and her façade begins crumbling before my eyes. It's not that Samantha hates me, I realize. She just doesn't want to face her own despicable behavior.

"Look, Sam. I was pissed at you for a long time. Really pissed. But I have the feeling you're going through a hard time. I know you were out with Scotch last week. Did something happen? It might help to talk to someone who's dealt with him before."

Samantha looks up at the ceiling and fans her face like she does when she's trying not to cry. I duck into one of the stalls and grab a bit of toilet paper. Wordlessly, I hold it out to her, like a peace treaty.

She accepts it.

Turning toward the sink, she blows her nose. Then she leans forward and stares at herself while she speaks. "There was a bonfire Thursday night. Everybody was there." Her eyes flicker toward me. "Well, you know what I mean."

I shrug. A bonfire with a bunch of cheerleaders and

football players sounds kind of like the ninth circle of hell to me.

"Scotch asked me to go with him. I don't know why I said yes—I guess I was still a little mad about you going to the dance with him last year. It's like I had to prove something to myself—that he wanted me. Or something. It was dumb. Anyway, I chugged, like, four beers. And then I started to feel sick. I puked in the weeds, and Scotch held my hair. He was being really sweet. I remember getting in the car with him to go home, but nothing after that. When I woke up, I was propped against my front door. He just left me there, I guess . . ."

Sam stops for a moment and then looks at me in the mirror. "Vee, I didn't have any underwear on." She crosses her arms over her chest and starts to cry. "I looked everywhere and couldn't find them. On Friday morning, I heard some guys talking about how Scotch was saying I slept with him. And that he had proof."

I stand for a moment, not really knowing what to do. I can count the number of times I've seen Samantha cry on one hand. Even when we were best friends, she liked to pretend that she was invincible. I remember when her older brother had an emergency appendectomy, I went to visit Sam at the hospital. Her eyes remained dry the whole time I was there. I kind of wanted her protective shell to break, so I could be there for her and comfort her. But now that I have the chance, I feel totally lost.

"Holy shit, Samantha," I say. My words feel stupid and worthless, but they seem to break through to her, just the same. She holds her arms out to me, and I bridge the gap between us to give her a long hug.

"I just wish I knew what happened," she whispers.

"I know the feeling," I say, thinking back to my own encounter with Scotch. To this day, it sickens me to know that he was alone with my unconscious body. He could have done whatever he wanted if Rollins hadn't burst into the locker room.

Samantha pulls back and looks me in the eye. "I'm sorry about that night." She doesn't need to say which one. We're both thinking back to Homecoming last year. I confronted her after the dance, accusing her of watching Scotch drag me down to the locker room. She never knew how I knew. The truth was I slid into her and saw the whole scene through her eyes. She never denied knowing about what happened to me, though. And she never apologized. Until now.

"I was so angry with you," she says. "You knew how much I liked him. I—I kind of felt like you deserved what happened. And now I know I was wrong. No one deserves that. No one. I'm so, so sorry."

Looking into her eyes, I know that Samantha's being genuine. She feels terrible about what happened to me. Just like I'm sick over what happened to her.

"He's an asshole," I say simply.

She backs away from me and takes a deep breath. "That's an understatement. I just wish there were some way to get back at him."

The wheels in my brain start turning. I remember a

novel I read once in which a girl pretended to make out with a guy in his car. She waited until he was completely naked, and then she stole his car, leaving him to walk home in the buff.

Lightbulb.

"Hey, Sam. I have an idea."

She sniffs. "What?"

My scheme is still not fully formed in my head. Of course Scotch wouldn't believe Samantha or I would want to get together with him—not after what he did to us. We need someone else. Someone Scotch would like. A cheerleader.

Regina.

I clap my hands together. "Come over after cheerleading practice. Bring Regina. I have the best plan ever!"

"Does your plan involve supergluing his privates to the wall?"

I laugh. "No. It's even better."

She smiles, but I can sense there's something more she wants to say. She shuffles her feet, looking as though she's searching for the right words. "Hey, Vee?"

"Yeah?"

"I never did thank you for what you did for me during the fire. I know that you risked your own life, trying to pull me out. I don't know if I'd have been able to do the same thing."

I study her face. It feels good to look at her and recognize the girl I see looking back at me. "You would have. I know it."

She reaches out and squeezes my hand. "Well, I guess I'll see you tonight." She crosses the bathroom and puts her hand on the door, getting ready to leave.

"Wait a sec," I say. "I'll make sure those guys are gone."

I duck my head outside, and sure enough, the two boys have disappeared. I motion for Samantha to follow me, and we return to our lockers. I grab my backpack and hoodie and then turn to find Samantha standing in front of her open locker door, staring at herself in the mirror.

"I can't go to practice. All the girls will be talking about what I supposedly did with Scotch."

I grab the tube of fuchsia lipstick from the shelf in her locker and hand it to her. "Of course you can, silly. You're Samantha Phillips." She takes the tube from me and holds it for a moment, feeling the weight of it. She uncaps it, swipes it across her lips, and returns it to its place on the shelf. As she presses her lips together, I think that only Samantha Phillips would have the balls to wear lipstick in such a bright shade of pink. She slams the locker door.

"You're right. I am." She gives me a shaky smile and then turns to head to the gym. I watch her walking away, her head held high.

Samantha, Mattie, and Regina show up a little after five.

Mattie does a belly flop onto my bed, and Samantha perches shyly on the rocking chair in the corner of my room. It feels so strange to have her in my bedroom after more than a year. Mattie keeps giving us curious looks, no doubt wondering why I invited Samantha and Regina over.

Regina wanders over to my desk and sits down. She picks up a framed picture of me and Mattie on the beach and sighs. "Is this at Lake Okoboji? My parents took Todd and me there every summer when we were little. We had so much fun."

I gently take the picture out of her hands. "Did Samantha tell you guys what Scotch did to her?"

Mattie winces. "What an asshole."

I examine Regina's face, looking for confirmation that she's disturbed enough by Scotch's actions that she'll help us with my plan. She scowls. "Yeah. I can't believe he'd do something like that."

"Well," I tell her, "if you help us, we can get him back."

"What can *I* do to help?"

"We're going to teach Scotch a little lesson. And we need your help."

"Why me?" Regina asks.

"He likes cheerleaders," I say. "Obviously he's not going to go for me or Mattie. He knows we both despise him. And he'd be too suspicious if Samantha came onto him, after what he did. We need someone younger, someone he'll *think* he has the upper hand with . . ." I look at Regina, thinking how perfect she is for the part. Her hair is long and soft, falling around her face in light brown curls. Her heart-shaped face is bare except for a hint of lip gloss and mascara. She looks so innocent. Scotch would never suspect she'd be a part of a plan to take him down. "All we need you to do is ask him to take you to Lookout Point tomorrow night. Say you've been admiring him all year long, and you'd like a chance to get to know him better."

Regina blushes. "I can't say that."

"Sure you can," Samantha cuts in. "Just call on your inner vixen."

"My inner *what*?"

"Your inner vixen," Samantha says, tossing her hair. "It's what I always do when I'm feeling less than confident. I ask what my inner vixen would do. She always gives me the courage to be the strongest woman I can be."

"So what's the rest of the plan?" Mattie asks, anxious to get back to business. "Regina gets Scotch up to Lookout Point, and then what?"

"All Regina will have to do is get him up there. Then she'll get out of the car and find Samantha, who will be waiting by the old pavilion. I'll take care of the rest."

The three girls stare, waiting for me to go on.

"What are you going to do to him?" Mattie demands.

"Get him naked and leave him stranded."

"How are you going to get him naked?" Samantha demands.

"You just leave that up to me," I say mysteriously, thinking about how easy it'll be to slide into Scotch, undress him, toss his clothes off the side of the cliff, and then leave him to find his way back to town, naked as the day he was born.

Scotch will get just what he deserves.

I wander into the hall, heading for the bathroom to wash my face and brush my teeth before bed. Mattie is downstairs with my dad, watching *MythBusters*.

I notice that my father's door is standing open. I see a shadow moving inside. It's certainly not my dad, whose laughter I hear booming from below. It has to be Lydia.

I tiptoe right up to the threshold and peek around the corner. Lydia is standing before my father's bureau with her back to me, but I can see her reflection in my mother's antique mirror. She's got the top drawer open and is sifting through his underwear and socks.

What exactly does she think she's doing?

In awe, I watch as Lydia retrieves a small velvet box from the drawer. She holds it reverently in her hand for a moment, caressing it with her eyes. Then she lifts the top and looks inside.

It's my mother's wedding ring.

My father has kept it hidden away in his drawer for years. Sometimes, when I was younger, I'd sneak into his room and pull it out. I even put it on once in a while and danced around the house, pretending to be her. My mother.

But what could Lydia possibly want with my mother's ring?

And how did she even know where to find it?

I duck out of the room and lean against the wall, my heart pounding. I don't know what Lydia is doing in our house. I don't know what her intentions are. But I swear to myself that I will find out.

I hear a drawer slam shut inside the room, so I race down the hallway. I casually act as though I'm coming out of my room and heading to the bathroom when Lydia comes out of my dad's room and shuts the door.

"Oh," she says when she sees me. "I was just putting away some laundry."

She beams at me, and all I can think is that I've never seen a more fake smile in my entire life.

CHAPTER TWELVE

I'm sitting in Mrs. Winger's room, waiting for class to begin. Samantha swoops in and sits next to me. "Wait until you see Regina," she says wickedly.

"What did you do?" My stomach is in knots as I go over our plan in my head.

"I helped her get in touch with her inner vixen," she says. "There's no way Scotch will turn her down."

At that moment, the bell rings, and Mrs. Winger claps to get everyone's attention. Samantha slides out of the seat next to me and crosses the room to sit at her own desk. Throughout the period, Samantha keeps looking my way and smiling mischievously.

After class, she grabs my elbow and steers me toward the freshman hallway. I see a cluster of freshman girls, and in the middle is one I barely recognize. Samantha has straightened Regina's curly hair, giving her a more sophisticated look. Instead of the barely-there lip gloss and mascara, Samantha has lined Regina's eyes with a pencil as black as coal and stained her lips a dark red.

I realize Samantha loaned Regina some of her clothes. A black miniskirt and a tight tank top with spaghetti straps. She's wearing strappy black sandals on her feet. She looks like she's at least nineteen. She'll be lucky if she goes an hour without getting busted for violating dress code.

"Doesn't she look great?" Samantha dances around. The girls surrounding Regina agree, telling Samantha what a fantastic job she did and all demanding that they get the next makeover.

"How do you feel?" I ask Regina.

Her eyes are wide, but she shakes her head slightly and I can almost hear her calling on her inner vixen. "I feel good. Let's do this." She's looking over my shoulder at someone down the hall. When I turn, I see Scotch sauntering toward us with one of his football buddies.

"Are you sure?" I ask.

Regina takes a deep breath and risks a look at Samantha, who claps her on the back. "Definitely."

She pushes past me, as if she's afraid to wait a second longer in case her determination fades. The group of girls that had gathered around her watches her glide through the hallway and up to Scotch Becker. Sam and I duck around the corner and peek out. I can't hear what she says, but Scotch looks down at her, transfixed. The guy he was walking with yawns and salutes Scotch before disappearing into a classroom.

It seems Samantha's handiwork has paid off when Scotch pulls out his phone and appears to enter Regina's number. Then he leans down and whispers something in her ear.

She flashes him a big smile, then turns and comes back toward us. Scotch deposits his phone back into his pocket and disappears into the classroom.

"So?" Samantha demands when Regina returns.

"It's a date," Regina says. I can't help but notice that her face is a little pale, despite the foundation Samantha caked onto it. A twinge of guilt passes through me, but then I remind myself that I'm not just doing this for the girls who Scotch has already hurt. It's for Regina, too, and all the girls he might hurt in the future.

"It's a date," Samantha repeats and then holds her hand up for a high five. It takes me a minute, but then I smack her hand with my own.

After school, I get my backpack from my locker and head down the hall to meet up with Rollins. I'm not sure whether I want to tell him about tonight's plan. He'll have his radio show, and I don't want him to worry about me all night when he's supposed to be concentrating. I'm sure he'd try to stop me if he knew, say it was too dangerous or something. The best thing would be to wait until it's already done and I'm home safe. Then we can laugh about it together.

I slow down when I spot Rollins. He's talking to Anna. I stop and watch. It's painful to see them leaning together and laughing. She reaches out and touches his arm, shaking her gorgeous black hair back from her face. He bends down and whispers something in her ear, causing her to erupt in another earthquake of giggles, shaking her ample chest beneath her top.

I feel sick.

Before either one can look in my direction, I spin around and speed-walk in the other direction. I pass the bathrooms and the main office, and take the far exit so I won't risk running into Rollins and Anna in the parking lot.

It's been a long while since I walked home alone. In fact, I can't remember the last time I didn't ride with Rollins. The path I usually walk, once so familiar, seems to take longer than I remember. I turn at the blue mailbox and watch my feet as they carry me toward home.

A yellow school bus passes me. I don't look up.

Finally, I reach my street. The houses all look dark and empty. Even though it's spring, the afternoon is gray, and everything seems muddy and drab.

I cheer slightly when I see that Lydia's car isn't in our driveway.

Hurrying up the sidewalk, I reach into the pocket of my hoodie to pull out my house key. As I slip it into the lock, something blurs in the corner of my eye. I turn my head quickly and see a blue station wagon at the intersection a few houses down. It pauses at the stop sign and then continues on.

Behind the wheel is a woman with her hair pulled into a bun.

Before I know it, the car has disappeared.

It's a coincidence, I tell myself.

There are probably plenty of women with buns in Iowa City, driving blue station wagons, creeping by my house.

Stop it. You know it was her.

Diane.

If I'd been thinking straight, I would have looked at her license plate, memorized the numbers and letters. I could have slid into Officer Teahen at the police station and had one of the secretaries look up the woman's last name and address.

But it all happened too fast.

Next time I see her, I will be prepared.

But I'm hoping there won't be a next time.

CHAPTER THIRTEEN

Approximately an hour before Regina and Scotch are supposed to meet up, I am standing in my room, pulling a black T-shirt over my head. I've also found a black wool cap to pull over my blond hair to make sure no one will see me.

"So what's the plan again?" I ask Mattie, prompting her to repeat the details we've gone over several times already.

"I'll tell Dad you weren't feeling well and went to bed early." She glances over at the blankets on my bed, which I've arranged to look like a sleeping body. "Sorry, Vee, but it's all over if he comes in here. That doesn't look like you at all."

"Then don't let him come in here," I say. "Make it believable."

She frowns. "I wish I were going with you. This job sucks."

"Look," I say. "I'll tell you everything as soon as I get home. It'll be just like you were there."

She crosses her arms and taps her foot.

"Hey. Do you want me and Rollins to go to the movie with you and Russ this weekend or not? Dad won't let you go otherwise."

Mattie glares. "That's low."

"Come on. I need you here."

She sighs and finally says, "Okay. Fine. Just make sure you're not too late."

I give her a quick hug. "Thanks, Matt. Okay, you know what to do."

Mattie grabs her math homework and opens the bedroom door. I follow her downstairs. She takes a right and goes into the living room, where Dad and Lydia are watching TV. I hear Mattie loudly ask my father if he could help her with an equation, and I take advantage of that moment to slip out the front door.

Samantha is waiting a few houses down, as we planned, her car idling.

"Shall we?" she asks, putting the car into drive.

"Let's go," I reply.

We reach our destination a few minutes before ten. Samantha parks her car next to the crumbling pavilion, and I get out and hike the rest of the way to Lookout Point. I find a small grove of trees not far from the spot where kids park. I sit down beneath a tree to wait, feeling the small piece of cloth I tore from last year's Homecoming dress tucked away in my pocket. I've used it before to slide into his head.

Five minutes pass, and I wonder if Scotch and Regina

are going to come after all. I panic as I consider the possibility that Scotch could have taken her somewhere else, and she'd be alone with him.

They're ten minutes late.

Fifteen.

I'm just about ready to go find Samantha and suggest that we call Regina when some headlights flash through the trees above my head. The familiar sight of Scotch's Mustang crunches by on the gravel, and the car stops about twenty yards from my hiding spot, facing the city lights.

I squint, trying to see what's going on, but all I can really make out is the back of Scotch's head and Regina's profile. They seem to be lost in conversation. After a few minutes, Scotch leans toward Regina.

What are you doing, Regina? You're supposed to get out of the car.

I decide I can't wait any longer.

Lying down, I rub my fingers against the fabric, concentrating on the sensation of silk against skin. The whole world starts to fade away, and then I am gone.

The car smells of liquor and leather.

Scotch hoists a bottle and takes a huge drink. The liquid burns all the way down. He looks over at Regina, who's gazing at him with bedroom eyes. Perhaps she has been drinking, too. This plan isn't going to work if Regina *wants* to make out with Scotch. She doesn't know him, doesn't know what he's capable of.

"I'm just . . . so fragile right now," Scotch says.

The line makes me want to gag.

Regina reaches over and grabs his hand. "It's going to be okay. You know, after my brother died—"

How am I going to pull this off if she doesn't leave?

Scotch leans toward Regina, cutting her off midsentence. I decide I've had enough. I take control of his limbs, his mouth. I yank him back into an upright position.

"Are you okay?" Regina asks, her eyes wide.

"Get out of here," I tell her.

"Excuse me?"

"I said to get out of here," I repeat, more loudly this time. She scrambles backward, fumbling with the door handle. It takes her several tries, but she finally pushes open the door and bursts into the cool night. She doesn't even bother to close the door, just starts running.

Shit.

I didn't mean to scare her.

Then I notice that Scotch's keys are dangling from the ignition. I'll throw them off the cliff, along with his clothes. Then he'll have to walk home butt-naked.

A movement catches my eye. Something in the headlights. Someone.

At first glance, I think it's my sister, and I'm ready to get out of the car and yell at her for not staying at home like I told her to, but then I remember I'm in Scotch's body.

The girl turns, light bouncing off her blond hair, and I realize it isn't my sister. The black Nine Inch Nails T-shirt. The torn jeans. It's what I'm wearing, or what I was wearing before I slid into Scotch.

The girl.

Is.

Me.

Unable to breathe, I push the car door open. The girl is twirling around, inches from the cliff. Doesn't she know she's close to falling?

As I watch her, something occurs to me. If I am here, inside Scotch . . . that means someone else is inside me. Making me dance so near the edge.

"Stop it!" I scream. My voice is deep. Scotch's voice.

The girl pauses. I take a step closer. Her gaze falls on me, and her eyes widen.

"Get away from the edge!" I yell, taking a few steps toward her.

She takes a step backward, closer to her death.

My death.

A fury takes hold of me. Who the hell does this person think she is, messing with my body? Twirling me on the edge of death? Staring at me like *I'm* the one doing wrong?

I reach out and grab her arm, try to pull her away from the edge.

Just then, I feel myself fading away.

I'm leaving Scotch's body.

No, not now.

But it's no use.

I'm gone.

CHAPTER FOURTEEN

I awake with my face in the dirt, my head pounding. It takes a moment for me to remember exactly what happened, but then it all comes rushing back. I push myself into a sitting position and look around. The headlights from the car illuminate the night. I don't see Scotch anywhere. Did he run away? I find it hard to believe he'd just leave his car behind.

My mind swims. What the hell just happened? One minute I'm ordering Regina to get out of the car so I can execute our plan of leaving Scotch stranded here naked, and the next minute I'm in a wrestling match with myself.

Struggling to my feet, I peer into the car.

There's no one.

"Scotch?" I call out, my voice unsure. I'm not really certain I want to find him. He isn't the smartest guy around, but he's intelligent enough to realize it's not a coincidence that I showed up the same night he brought Regina here. Still, the fact that he's disappeared into thin air gives me the creeps. I don't feel right leaving without knowing what happened to him.

A terrible thought pops into my head. I eye the edge of the cliff uneasily. Is it possible that, during our scuffle, Scotch fell over the precipice?

No. Please, no.

Moving slowly, as if in a dream, I approach the edge.

I don't want to look.

But I have to.

I stare down into the darkness.

There's something there.

A bit of white T-shirt.

A leg bent at an odd angle.

It's like my brain refuses to put all the pieces together. But they're all there. A puzzle of Scotch lying at the bottom of the cliff.

Broken.

Maybe dead.

Probably dead.

Minutes or hours later, I find myself wandering down the road in a daze. I almost walk past a car without noticing it before the driver starts blinking her headlights and honking. The window rolls down, and a familiar face materializes.

"What took you so long?" Samantha hisses. "Hurry up and get in the car." She stabs her thumb in the direction of the backseat. I follow her directions, opening the door and climbing inside. As soon as the door closes, she makes a U-turn and drives away.

Regina is sitting in the passenger seat. "You guys, I feel really bad for doing this to Scotch. Did you know his mother has lung cancer? He was really opening up to me."

Lung cancer. Is that what he was talking about in the car? That's why he was feeling so fragile? Maybe it wasn't just a line. God, I am such an asshole.

"Just because his mother has cancer doesn't make him any less of a douche," Samantha says. She glances at me in the rearview mirror. "How did it go?"

I look dully at her. The image of Scotch's mangled body looms before me. Suddenly, I become manic. "Stop the car! Stop the car! We have to go back!"

Samantha slams on the brakes. "Jesus, Vee. What's wrong with you?"

"We have to go back," I say. "Scotch is hurt. Maybe dead. We have to call 911. We have to get help."

Samantha stretches around to look at me. "What the hell are you talking about?"

I cradle my head in my hands. Samantha and Regina don't know about my sliding. How do I explain what happened? I end up telling half the truth, as it would have occurred if I were in my own body.

"I don't know," I say. "It's all kind of a blur. I was standing at the edge of the cliff, and Scotch came at me. And then . . . the next thing I remember is waking up on the ground. He must have fallen . . ."

"He fell?" Regina asks, her eyes wide. "How could Scotch just fall off a cliff?"

I stare at her in horror. She's right. It's very unlikely that Scotch, an athlete, would accidentally fall over the side. So what does this mean? Could whoever slid into me have pushed him? The thought makes me feel like puking.

Regina starts rocking back and forth and crying. I search for my phone and start to dial 911. Samantha reaches over the seat and grabs the phone out of my hand.

"You can't call the police," she says. "How are we going to explain what we were doing? If Scotch is dead, it's our fault. . . ." Her voice trails off, but the accusatory look she gives me makes her thoughts clear. If Scotch is dead, it's *my* fault.

Regina sobs even harder.

"But we have to get help," I say weakly.

Samantha's right, though. If we call the cops, they'll want to know what happened. What if they try to pin Scotch's fall on me? I cover my face with my hands.

Samantha grabs my wrist. "Vee, you've got to pull yourself together. I know you didn't mean for Scotch to fall, but that doesn't mean the police will see it that way. I don't want you to go to jail for this."

"I think I'm going to be sick," Regina says, and she pushes open her car door. I hear her retching into the weeds.

"What we need to do now is go home and act like nothing happened tonight. If anyone asks, we'll say we hung out at my place and watched movies. Jake is at college, and my parents are on a cruise, so no one will know we're lying."

I feel myself nodding. What Samantha is saying makes sense. Her parents are nice enough, but they're always going on some vacation and leaving her at home by herself. As long as the three of us vouch for one another, no one should get suspicious. It's the perfect alibi.

I rub my temples, my head aching.

What's wrong with me? I need an *alibi*?

"Regina. Did you hear what I just said?" Samantha demands.

Regina wipes her mouth. She doesn't say anything.

"Regina," Samantha repeats.

"We should call the police."

"Regina, get real," Samantha snaps. "Do you want Vee to go to prison?"

Regina cowers in her seat, not responding.

"I swear to God, Regina, if you say a word to anyone about what happened tonight, I will personally make your life a living hell." Samantha is seething, and I know better than to cross her when she's this angry.

Apparently Regina knows better, too, because she assents. "Okay, Samantha. I promise. I won't say anything. Okay? Are you happy now?"

"Tell me where we were tonight," Samantha orders.

"Your place. Watching movies." Regina won't look at either one of us. I wonder if she's telling the truth. Will she really keep this quiet, or is she just trying to appease Samantha?

I want to do the right thing. I want to call the police and tell them to send an ambulance right away because, even though I loathe Scotch Becker, he doesn't deserve to be lying in the dark. Dying. Or dead.

I always thought I was a strong person. A good person.

But, when it comes right down to it, I'm afraid this will be pinned on me. What if I go to prison for the rest of my life? For something I didn't mean to do?

I'm a coward.

I don't say anything.

"Okay, then." Samantha puts the car into gear. "Let's get out of here."

When I get home, Mattie is sprawled on my bed, fully clothed and snoring. I stare at her for a minute, wishing I could put off breaking the terrible news to her. I don't want to, but I have to tell Mattie. She's part of this, too.

I sit down on the bed beside her and gently shake her shoulder. "Mattie. Pssssst, Mattie, wake up!"

She stirs, and when she sees me, she bolts upright. "Ohmigod, you're back. Tell me everything. Don't leave out a single detail."

"Mattie," I say, and my somber tone quells her excitement. "Something bad happened. Something really bad."

She shakes her head. "What? Oh no. Did something happen to Regina?"

"Not to Regina," I say. "Something happened to Scotch."

I explain what happened. When I get to the part about him lying at the bottom of the cliff, Mattie puts her hand over her mouth. She looks like she's going to be sick.

"You're kidding, right?"

"Mattie, you know I'd never joke about something like this."

"Scotch is . . . dead?"

I think about Scotch, lying alone and cold at the bottom of the cliff, his limbs twisted in unnatural ways. He has to be dead. There's no way someone could survive that fall. "I'm pretty sure he is."

Thinking about Scotch, all alone in the middle of the night, his body turning stiff in the cold air, makes me feel ill. Suddenly, I don't care what happens to me. I can't just leave him there. I pull my phone out of my pocket.

"Wait, what are you doing?" Mattie asks.

"I'm calling the police."

"Don't," Mattie says, panicked. "Don't use your phone to call, Vee."

"I have to."

"Please," she says. "What if the police find out about our prank? We'll be in so much trouble. Let's just wait until tomorrow. We'll make an anonymous call. From somewhere it can't be traced to us."

I sigh. I can't stand to see Mattie so scared. Finally, I give in.

"Let's get some sleep."

She nods and lies down, but I know she'll be awake for the rest of the night.

Just like me.

We don't talk after that, but we both toss and turn into the early morning hours. I know we're both thinking about the body at the bottom of Lookout Point and wishing that we never, ever met Scotch Becker.

CHAPTER FIFTEEN

By the time I drag myself out of bed, Mattie has already gotten up. I look bleary-eyed at my alarm clock. Rollins will be here any minute.

All at once, the night before settles over me like a fog. I rush to the bathroom and throw up twice. After I rinse my face, I look at myself for a long time, wondering how I became a girl who could cover up a murder. Because if the person who slid into me pushed Scotch over the edge, and he is indeed dead . . . that's what I am, right? A murderer. At least, technically. Does it matter that I wasn't in my body when the crime was committed?

In my room, I pull on a pair of tattered jeans and a purple sweatshirt before going downstairs. Lydia and Mattie are sitting at the kitchen table. My father is nowhere to be seen. Mattie's hair is disheveled and she has deep circles under her eyes.

"Your dad had to leave early," Lydia explains. "I told him I'd take care of breakfast." She gestures to a place across from her. There's a plate loaded with bacon, eggs, and toast slathered with butter. It makes me feel like I'm going to be sick again. I grab a clean coffee cup from the cupboard and fill it to the brim, avoiding eye contact with Lydia. Screw my no-caffeine resolution, at least for today. I take a long drink.

"You look like you didn't sleep very well," Lydia observes.

I try to catch Mattie's gaze, but she looks away.

A car honks outside.

"It's Rollins," Mattie says. I get up without saying anything, grab my backpack, and follow Mattie out to the car.

"So did you listen last night? Seriously, like ten people called in. It was so amazing," Rollins says as he brakes at a stop sign. A couple of little kids with bright jackets walk in front of Rollins's car.

I haven't had time to think about what I'm going to tell Rollins. If my plan had worked out, I'd be giggling about how Scotch had to walk home in the nude. What would Rollins say if I told him the truth? That what was supposed to be a prank turned into a nightmare, ending in a horrific accident? I know that Rollins would do a lot to protect me, but would he keep this secret? Would I even want him to?

Mattie jumps in. "Vee actually went to bed early last night. She wasn't feeling well."

Rollins's eyes flicker toward me. "You okay?"

I cough. "Yeah, I'm fine. I was just tired. Sorry I missed your show."

"No problem." Rollins shrugs. "I'm glad you got some

rest. You've been looking kind of . . . um . . . haggard lately."

"Gee, thanks," I say.

In the school parking lot, Scotch's usual spot is empty. I can't stop staring at it. My sister spots Regina walking toward the school building and mumbles something about needing to talk to her. After she's gone, Rollins pulls the keys out of the ignition and slides them into his pocket.

"What's going on with you?" he asks quietly.

"What do you mean?"

"You just haven't been yourself lately. Is there something you want to talk about?"

In that moment, I'm filled with the need to spill everything that happened last night. It feels wrong to keep such a huge secret from Rollins, the guy who's been my closest friend for the last year.

But before I can answer, someone raps at Rollins's window. We both look over to see Anna standing next to the car, beaming at Rollins. Her hair is gleaming in the early morning light, and her cheeks are rosy from the fresh air.

Rollins shoots a look as if to say, *Last chance. Wanna talk?*

I turn away.

Rollins sighs and opens his door. "Hi, Anna."

"Hi, guys," she says brightly, smiling at Rollins and then me. "I'm not interrupting anything, am I?"

I shake my head vigorously. "Nope. Nothing. In fact, I've got to get inside. I forgot to do my Government homework. If I hurry, I've got just enough time to finish it before class starts." After spouting my lame excuse, I escape from the car and walk briskly toward the school. I hear Rollins calling my name, but I don't slow down.

Once inside, I start feeling sick again. I have to walk through the cafeteria to get to my locker, and the smell of rubbery eggs has me gagging. There are only a few lone souls eating breakfast.

The pay phone at the far end of the cafeteria catches my eye.

It's time.

I can't avoid it any longer.

I have to call the police.

Making sure no one is paying attention, I discreetly pick up the receiver with the sleeve of my shirt pulled over my hand, just in case the cops try to dust the phone for prints later, after they've found Scotch. Again, I wonder how I became this girl—someone who worries about leaving fingerprints.

Taking a deep breath, I dial the numbers.

9. 1. 1.

A woman answers, sounding not much older than me. "911. What is your emergency?"

I make my voice as low as it will go. "Yes, I'd like to report an accident at Lookout Point. Please send an ambulance." As soon as I finish, I hang up the phone and walk away as quickly as I can.

I head straight for the girls' restroom, hoping it's empty.

Inside, Regina stands in front of a sink. The faucet is running, but Regina isn't washing her hands. She's just staring at herself in the mirror. I know the look in her eyes, the haunted stare of someone who's overcome with shame.

"Hey," I say softly.

She doesn't respond.

I want to wrap my arms around her and tell her I know how she feels. It's like something out of a horror movie, to know someone might be dead and not be able to say a word about it. I want to tell her I couldn't fall asleep last night, either. I want to ease her mind. Before saying anything, though, I check beneath the stall doors to make sure no one's lurking, listening.

"I called the police from the cafeteria," I say. "They should be headed to Lookout Point right now."

Without looking at me, Regina turns off the water.

She pushes past me, her shoulder butting into mine. "Leave me the hell alone." With that, she disappears into the hallway.

Before English class, I see Samantha getting a drink of water. I stand behind her, waiting for her to finish. She jumps when she turns around.

"Jesus, you scared me."

"Sam, we have to talk about what happened."

Sam claps her hand over my mouth and looks around. "Not here."

I peel away her fingers. "But I have to tell you something." She may never forgive me for making that phone call, but she needs to know about it.

"Later," she insists.

The bell rings.

"Come on," Samantha says, hurrying across the hall to Mrs. Winger's classroom. "We're late."

Mrs. Winger doesn't say anything to Samantha or me as we dart to our desks. Instead, she passes out a story called "Young Goodman Brown" by Nathaniel Hawthorne. She tells us we'll want to pay special attention to the symbolism of different elements in the story that represent good and evil. I have no idea how I'm going to concentrate on the story.

She lets us pick partners to work with, so I wordlessly take the desk next to Samantha. *Partners in crime,* I can't help but think. She sits with her eyes glued to the badly photocopied story.

"Let's get this over with." Sam hunches over her desk and begins slowly reading aloud the story of Young Goodman Brown, a sort of regular guy who goes walking deep in the woods one night and comes across a dude I'm pretty sure is the devil. Brown sees all these people he knows from the village doing some kind of satanic ritual. The kicker is when he finds his own wife, Faith, participating.

"Duh, okay, so that's a symbol right there. His wife's name. Write it down. Faith. He lost his faith when he went walking with the devil." Samantha points at the empty notebook in front of me. I write down her suggestion.

It's hard to explain, but the story makes me feel really weird. I'm pretty sure it's about loss of innocence, and I can't help but feel like I went walking with the devil in the woods last night. Except I'm not sure if the devil was

Scotch or whoever slid into me or maybe even me, because I left a boy in a ditch to rot.

"Okay, put your desks in a circle for discussion," Mrs. Winger calls out. Everyone groans and maneuvers their desks to line the perimeter of the room. She draws a big T-chart on the board and asks for us to name some of the symbols we found.

"His wife," Samantha blurts. "She represents his faith."

"Okay," Mrs. Winger says, scribbling on the white-board with a dry-erase marker. "What else?"

"The dark man," someone else says. "Clearly he was the devil."

"Good," says Mrs. Winger. "Why do you think Goodman Brown went walking with the devil, even though he was supposedly a decent fellow?"

I speak up. "Because everyone walks with the devil at one point or another. Even Goodman Brown's perfect little wife, Faith, was hanging around with the rest of the townspeople in the forest, worshipping Satan. It just means that everyone makes bad choices in their lives. No one's perfect."

Especially not me, I think. *What if the hours I let pass before telling the police meant the difference between life and death for Scotch?*

Samantha looks over at me. "Yeah, but Goodman Brown let it destroy him. If he had just let it go, he would have been so much better off."

"Interesting," Mrs. Winger says, tapping the marker against her chin. "You girls really seem to have gotten into the story. I'm impressed."

The bell rings, and Mrs. Winger scrambles to pick up the photocopied stories.

Samantha and I stay in our seats, staring at each other for just a second. She passes her story to Mrs. Winger and then scoops up her books. She leaves the room without waiting for me.

CHAPTER SIXTEEN

The day seems to go on forever. Finally, the last bell rings. I trudge toward my locker, my textbooks feeling heavier than they normally do. It takes me three tries to get my locker open because my eyes keep blurring when I stare at the little numbers. I am beyond exhausted.

"So Regina is totally pissed." Mattie leans against the locker next to mine.

"I told her I called the police using the pay phone," I say wearily. "I don't know what else she wants me to do. Turn myself in?"

"She keeps talking about how Scotch was misunderstood and really was a good guy underneath it all."

"Ugh," I say. Though I feel bad that Scotch's mom has cancer, I'm fairly certain he's not a *good guy*.

"Pretty much. I'll try talking some sense into her at practice. Are you going straight home?"

"Yeah, I'll catch a ride with Rollins."

"Oh," Mattie says, her eyes getting all big like she knows something that I don't.

"What is it?"

"I just saw him walking out to the parking lot with Anna. I assumed you weren't riding with him."

My heart falls. I'd really been hoping for a chance to tell Rollins about what happened last night. I'm still not sure I did the right thing by calling the cops anonymously. I wanted to get his perspective because clearly Samantha isn't going to be a moral compass in this matter. And Mattie's too invested. She doesn't want to see me get in trouble.

I slam my locker door shut. "Great. I guess I'll walk. Again."

Mattie grabs my hand. "I'll see you when I get home." She lets go and hurries down the hallway, her ponytail bouncing.

I hoist my backpack onto my shoulders and somehow summon the energy to walk home. The sun is warm on my face, and it would be an enjoyable hike if it weren't for the morbid thoughts circling in my head. I keep wondering what's happening at Lookout Point. Did the paramedics, realizing that Scotch was nonresponsive, zip him into a body bag and load him onto a gurney? Are the police searching the woods for any evidence of foul play? Do Scotch's parents know yet?

When I turn onto my street, Lydia's yellow car in my driveway almost makes me want to turn around and run the other way. She's the last person I want to see right now, but I don't really have anywhere else to go. I turn the knob slowly and push open the front door. Inside, I hear nothing. After setting my backpack down and hanging up my jacket, I scope out the kitchen and living room. No one's there. I check out the upstairs. All the bedrooms are empty, and the bathroom door is wide open. No one is inside.

It appears that Lydia went out for the day. This piques my curiosity. Where would she go without her car?

I stand in the doorway to Mattie's room. The shades are drawn, painting the walls in darkness. I'm tempted to open them or turn on a light, but Mattie's window faces the driveway, and I don't want Lydia to realize someone is in here if she comes home early. I can make out a suitcase on the floor next to the closet, though, and I kneel down beside it.

My heart hammers in my chest. I grab the zipper and pull it open, exposing a bunch of wadded-up clothes. One thing is for sure: my aunt isn't the neatest person in the world. I recognize the outfit she wore when she showed up at the front door. It's damp and shoved into a corner of the suitcase. Poking through the clothes doesn't reveal more than my aunt's preference for black silk underwear, unfortunately.

I push the clothes back into the suitcase and zip it up, noticing a pocket on the front that I hadn't seen before. From the bulge, I'm able to tell there's definitely something inside. Excited, I yank open the zipper and thrust my hand in. My fingers close around a leather wallet. Bingo. I pull it out so I can examine it properly.

Inside, I find a wad of receipts from places in San Francisco. A few credit cards. And her driver's license. All of these items have the same name on them, but they're not my aunt's name. They say "Lila Harrington."

Who is Lila Harrington?

That's when I hear the front door open.

Crap crap crap crap crap.

My dad's at work, and Mattie's at cheerleading practice, meaning there's only one other person who'd be walking into our house.

Lydia.

My panic makes me uncoordinated, and I struggle with stuffing the wallet back into the suitcase pocket. It takes me several tries to zip it up. I scramble to my feet and am poised to race out the door when something on the bureau catches my eye.

It is the picture of my mother in a sombrero.

The one I thought I lost last Thursday, before I got into the car accident.

I hear footsteps on the stairs, and the sound is enough to shake me out of my paralysis. I rush out of the room, pulling the door shut behind me. Somehow I make it to my doorway and bolt inside.

Lydia comes down the hall and pauses outside my room. "Hello, Vee."

I'm out of breath. "Huh–hi. How was your day?"

"It was great." She ticks off her daily activities on her fingers. "Took a walk around the neighborhood this morning. Lovely houses. Had a late lunch at this cute diner. They had the best pie. Seriously. I'll have to take you there sometime. Then I walked around downtown and did some window-shopping." She sighs. "The weather is just perfect today, don't you think?"

"Perfect," I agree, hoping she doesn't see the way my smile wobbles.

Her face turns more serious. "I was hoping we could have a little talk."

"Um, okay."

Lydia shifts her weight, looking uncomfortable. "I want you to know I didn't say anything to your father about you coming in late last night."

My heart pounds. "What are you talking about? I went to sleep early."

She gives me a long look. "Right."

"What? Don't you believe me?"

"I wasn't exactly born yesterday, Vee."

We stare at each other.

If she was the one who slid into me before Scotch's accident, of course she would know I wasn't in my bed.

After a long moment, Lydia says, "So you weren't out with that boy? Rollins?"

"No," I sputter, confused. "I told you. I wasn't feeling well. I was in bed."

She sighs. "Look, are you at least using protection?" The maternal tone she uses makes me want to vomit. Who does she think she is, anyway?

"I'm not having sex," I say. "Not that it's any of your business."

"Promise me," she says. "Promise me that if you do have sex, you'll use protection. I'll even take you to Planned Parenthood if you want. We can get you on the pill."

"Jesus. What's your problem?"

She takes a few steps into my room, puts her hand on my shoulder. "I just want to be here for you. I've been without a real family for so long. I want to be a good aunt to you. Vee, if there's anything you need, don't hesitate to ask."

She pats me on the back, and I feel all my muscles tense. She sighs and backs away from me. "See you at dinner."

"Wait," I say, thinking of the picture I saw in her room. I want some confirmation that Lydia's as shady as I think she is. "Have you seen a picture of my mother lying around anywhere? She's wearing a sombrero. It's from her honeymoon."

Is my mind playing tricks on me, or did Lydia's muscles just tighten, ever so slightly?

She crosses her arms over her chest. "Sure, I saw that picture. It was lying on the floor under the couch downstairs. I held on to it for a little while. Is it yours?"

I hold her gaze. She doesn't look away.

"Do you want it? I can go get it for you," Lydia offers.

"Yes, please."

I hold my breath as she walks down the hallway. Doing the math in my head, I realize the last time I saw the picture was at breakfast on Thursday morning. It was missing by suppertime that night. What if Lydia is lying about finding it underneath the couch? Is it possible she was following me the day I lost it? Could I have dropped it in the parking lot or something? If so, Lydia could have slid into me that night and forced me to steal my father's car, hoping

I would get into an accident. But then, seeing I wasn't hurt badly enough, she could have taken her plan a step further and decided to infiltrate our home. To destroy us from the inside out.

This speculation makes me feel crazy.

Still, when Lydia returns with the picture and presses it into my hand, I see an arch in her eyebrow that makes me wonder if I'm not.

CHAPTER SEVENTEEN

After dinner, I try to concentrate on my homework, but it's no use. I put away my Introduction to Psychology textbook after reading the same page six times in a row and not comprehending any of the material.

I hear Lydia laughing downstairs.

What does she want from us? What was she doing with the picture of my mother?

My gaze falls on my laptop. Nothing came up when I searched for my aunt under her real name, but maybe that's because she's been using a pseudonym.

I get up and lock my door.

Sitting back on my bed, my computer on my lap, I pull up Google. In a moment of inspiration, I type in "Lila Harrington," along with "San Francisco, California."

A few dozen hits.

I click on the first one. It's the faculty page for a high school in San Francisco. One of the teachers listed is Lila Harrington. I click on the link and see a picture of my aunt. She wears a pearl necklace and a half smile. According to the page, she has taught art at the school for the last five years. I wonder what the school is doing for a replacement in the middle of April. Did she tell the school she was taking a break, or did she just not show up one day?

Backtracking to my Google results page, I click on the next entry down. It's an engagement announcement for Lila Harrington and James Sutton that appeared in the *San Francisco Chronicle* in late October. I scroll down and scan the biographical details about the couple. The article says that Lila comes from Iowa and has lived in California for twenty years. She received her degree in education from UCLA thirteen years ago and spent three years teaching at a school in northern California before taking a position at her current school. She enjoys rock climbing and pottery.

Lila met James while camping last summer. She describes the experience as "love at first sight" and knew that she'd spend the rest of her life with him. I roll my eyes. Farther down the page, there is a picture of the two of them. James is incredibly good-looking and muscular. He kind of reminds me of Brad Pitt. I wonder if Lydia told him about her family, who she abandoned years ago. At Christmastime, did he wonder why she didn't have anyone to spend the holidays with?

I stare at the picture of the two of them. If only I could speak with him, he'd be able to provide so many answers. Navigating to an online phone book, I wonder, *Why not?* If I can find his number, why shouldn't I call him and ask him what he knows about my aunt?

I find three listings for J. Sutton. Only one is under age

forty, though, and James definitely doesn't look much older than Lydia. *That has to be him,* I think, digging my phone out of my pocket.

I punch his number into my phone and hit the Call button.

"Hello?"

"Uh, hi," I say, breathing hard. I probably should have put some thought into what I was going to say before I actually made the call. The poor guy will think I'm some pervert mouth breather.

"Who is this?"

"Hi," I say again, cringing. "Um, my name is Sylvia Bell. I'm looking for Lila Harrington . . ."

His voice turns sharp. "Who did you say this was?"

I cough. "My name is Sylvia Bell."

"Is this another reporter? I've already said everything I know. We were supposed to be married last Saturday, and she disappeared. Look, I'm really getting sick of this *Runaway Bride* bullshit. Something bad must have happened to her. Don't you people understand?"

I am quiet.

So Lydia ditched her wedding to come to Iowa. Why would she do that? What happened to make her leave her life in California? One thing is clear. This man doesn't know anything about her real life. He sounds genuinely broken, like he believes his wife-to-be has been kidnapped or something.

"I'm sorry, Mr. Sutton. I'm sure Lila is fine, wherever she is."

I hear him sob on the other end. "No, she's not fine. If she were fine, she would be here. With me."

I hit the End Call button and drop my head into my hands.

Who *is* this woman?

Mattie gets home around five. I sit on my bed, watching her unbraid her hair in front of my full-length mirror.

"Lydia said she had a little talk with you," Mattie says, examining her face for blemishes.

I consider telling Mattie what I've learned about Lydia. But she doesn't know about sliding, so it would be hard for me to explain why I felt the need to go through Lydia's things. My theory that Lydia has been sliding into me sounds insane, even to me.

"Yeah," I say, rolling my eyes. "She thinks I'm on the verge of getting pregnant or something. It was weird, considering I don't even have a boyfriend."

"She can tell something's going on. She just doesn't know what it is. She's trying to help."

I shake my head. "When did you get so buddy-buddy with her?"

Mattie turns toward me. "We did a lot of talking last night. She told me all she wants is a family. She was lonely in California."

"She could have had a family if she didn't run away. It's not our fault she's been off doing God knows what for the past twenty years," I say, closing my hands into fists. "It's like she's just decided to leech on to our family instead of making her own."

Mattie's face turns hard. "I'm going to take a shower."

She makes it halfway out the door before she turns back and says, "I can't believe you could be so cruel to our own flesh and blood."

After Mattie slams the door, I flop back onto my bed and glare at the ceiling. *If only it were so simple,* I think. I envy Mattie, being able to open her arms and accept someone new into her life without suspicion.

Once, in school, we had this discussion about whether ignorance really is bliss. Everyone kept saying they'd rather know the truth than go on living a lie. But me, I just kept arguing that the only way to truly be happy is to *not* know the truth.

Because the truth is too complicated.

And, most of the time, the truth is too ugly.

CHAPTER EIGHTEEN

I'm on my way to the bathroom when I notice that Mattie's door is ajar. Soft voices escape into the hall. Through the crack, I can see Mattie sitting on the bed. Lydia sits behind her, pulling a hairbrush through my sister's long, blond tresses.

"Your hair is so much like your mother's," Lydia says.

"Yeah?" I can hear the pride in my sister's voice.

"Mmmmhmmm. Your mother had the most beautiful, silky hair. I was so jealous. Mine frizzes up at the mere mention of rain, but your mother's hair always behaved."

Mattie sighs. "Can you tell me a story about her?"

I lean against the wall, barely breathing.

"Let's see," Lydia replies. She combs through Mattie's hair thoughtfully. "Well, when we were little girls, your grandparents took us up to Lake Okoboji for a week every summer. Even though it was expensive, we always rented a boat. One of us would go out waterskiing with your grandfather, and the other would stay on the dock, sunbathing with your grandmother. We took turns."

"Anyway, there was one summer . . . Your mom must have been about twelve. She was out skiing, and I was sitting on the dock, reading some terrible fashion magazine. I happened to look up, and I noticed that I couldn't see your mom. Your grandfather was out there on the boat, zipping around, but I couldn't see anyone on the skis behind him. Well, I stood up and started shouting at him, trying to get his attention. After a minute or so, he turned around and saw that Susan was down. Thank God she was wearing a life jacket, or he never would have found her."

I let out a puff of air.

"Wow," Mattie says. "So Mom just passed out? Did she do that a lot? That must be where Vee gets it from."

"She was never diagnosed," Lydia says, setting the hairbrush on the bed. "But I strongly suspect she had narcolepsy."

"That's one trait I'm glad I didn't inherit," Mattie says.

I back away and duck into the bathroom, locking the door. When I look in the mirror, I realize that I've been crying.

Later, I am sitting in my mother's rocking chair in the corner of my room, a blanket draped around my shoulders. I think about the story Lydia was telling Mattie.

It sounds like my mother definitely struggled with the same condition that I have. I wonder if it was as torturous to her as it is to me. If she was always learning things she didn't want to know. If she longed to just be normal.

I roll onto my side and prop my head up with my hand. My eyes fall on the clothes I wore last night, and my thoughts turn to Scotch. Did the police figure out who he was with? Did they find our footsteps in the dirt? Can they tell there was a scuffle? If only there were some way to find out what's going on.

I stop rocking.

There *is* a way.

Back in October, when I was investigating Sophie's death, I picked up a glove that Scotch dropped. I thought I could use it to slide into him and find out if he was Sophie's killer. But when I used the glove, I didn't slide into Scotch. I slid into his *father*. The glove belonged to his dad. Somehow, I knew better than to throw it away. I stashed the glove in my bottom drawer, beneath my collection of concert T-shirts.

I jump up and rush over to my chest of drawers. I throw T-shirts everywhere in my hurry to find the glove. There it is, at the very bottom. I seize it and slam the drawer shut.

I shut my door and then return to my bed. For a moment, I just stare at the glove. Do I really want to do this? Do I want to slide into the man whose son's death I might be responsible for?

I don't have a choice.

I have to know what's going on.

Ignorance is not an option anymore.

Heart pounding, I lay my fingers on the glove, rubbing it softly. The room starts to fade away. I let go of myself.

I'm sitting in the cab of a pickup truck, driving down a busy street.

The driver carefully navigates through traffic, letting his foot slowly lower onto the brake when he sees a yellow light up ahead.

A phone on the seat beside me buzzes.

When the light turns red, he answers the call. "Hello?" he says gruffly, glancing in the rearview mirror. I've never seen Scotch's father before, but he looks like his son, except for the worn, leathery quality of his skin and the receding hairline.

Someone is sobbing on the other end of the phone. I can't make out what the person is saying. "Calm down," he says gently. "What's going on?"

"Honey, the police are here," a woman finally gasps. "Please. Come home."

I awaken abruptly. Mattie is above me, holding my shoulders, shaking me. When she sees that I'm conscious, she breathes a sigh of relief. "Are you okay? You passed out. Why are you holding this dirty old glove?"

I crumple the glove into a ball and hide it behind my back, thinking belatedly that will only make Mattie more curious. "What?" I ask stupidly.

"Rollins is on the phone," Mattie says, holding it out.

I accept the phone and bring it to my ear. "Rollins?"

He coughs. "Hey, I looked for you after school. I'm getting the feeling that you're avoiding me."

Mattie watches me curiously. I shoo her out of the room.

Switching the phone to my opposite ear, I try to think of something to say, anything other than the truth—which is that I don't want to hang out with Anna.

"I've just . . . had a lot on my mind."

"Is this about your aunt?" Rollins asks.

I get off my bed, walk over to the door, and peek out to make sure no one is listening. "I'd rather not talk about it right now. Tomorrow?" I push the door closed, but even then I'm paranoid about Lydia hearing our conversation.

He's quiet for a moment. Finally he says, "Sure. I guess."

I know that tone of voice. Rollins is pissed that I won't open up to him. But there's not much I can do about it now.

"Okay, I'll see you tomorrow morning," I say, and then I push End Call.

Where was I?

Picking up the crumpled glove from my bed, I remember Scotch's father's phone call. My heart starts to pound as I remember his wife's words: *Honey, the police are here. Come home.*

This time I lock the door.

I'm sitting in the living room in Scotch's house. His mother, wearing a bandanna on her head, sits next to me. I recall what Regina said about his mother having lung cancer and feel terrible. This woman has been through enough. Should she have to bury her son, too?

Sitting across from us is Officer Teahen, the policeman

who investigated Sophie's murder. I actually haven't seen him since he came to our door to tell us about Zane's accident. He looks like he's aged since then. Lines have appeared around his eyes and mouth. I wonder how many of them are due to dead teenagers.

Officer Teahen speaks. "Do you remember the name of the girl he said he was going out with?"

I feel Scotch's father shake his head. "He dates a different girl every week, almost. There's no way we can keep track of them all." I'm not sure if it's my imagination, but there's a slight undertone of pride in the man's voice that makes me feel ill. Still, I'm glad that Regina's name doesn't come up. She'd crumble if she had to talk to the cops.

"We're wondering if the girl who made the call from the school today is the same one Scott went out with last night. Tomorrow we'll send an officer to ask around and see if Scott mentioned his date to any of his friends."

Scotch's mother coughs into a Kleenex. I see a splotch of blood on it. "I don't understand why the girl didn't call *last night*. Just thinking of my boy, lying there, all by himself . . ."

I have never felt guiltier in my life.

"My guess is that she's afraid of getting busted for underage drinking. We found a bottle of rum in Scott's car."

Scotch's father curses.

His mother speaks again, her voice getting louder than I'd ever guessed it could. "Who would care about getting a ticket for underage drinking when a boy's life is at stake? He could have died last night."

Huh?

Hold everything.

Is Scotch *alive*?

For a moment I feel relief. But then the implications of this possibility swirl around my head. If Scotch is still alive, did he see what happened before he fell? Did he see *me*?

"I agree, it's a very strange situation. But sometimes teenagers don't make very rational decisions," Officer Teahen says. "Luckily, the paramedics got there in time. I understand your son is in stable condition."

"Yeah, no thanks to the bitch who left him there," Scotch's father says.

Scotch's mother starts to cry. His father scoots closer to her and takes her hand. He speaks sternly to the officer. "I think my wife has had enough. Can we cut this conversation short?"

Officer Teahen, looking like he would very much mind cutting the conversation short, opens his mouth, seems to think better of it, and then shuts it again. "Of course. We'll be in touch as soon as we have more information."

The two men stand and shake hands. The officer walks to the front door, gives a polite nod, and then shows himself out.

Scotch's father settles back down with his wife, who is doubled up and coughing into her handkerchief. He pushes her hair out of her eyes tenderly. "It's okay, honey. It's all going to be okay."

———

Someone knocks on my door. I glance at my clock and note my father won't be home for another hour or so. I heave a sigh and open the door, expecting Mattie to be on the other side, ready for another round.

But it isn't Mattie.

It's Lydia.

Her face is grave.

"Something has happened," she says.

I don't move. Don't speak.

"You should probably be sitting down for this."

I shuffle toward my bed and pull the comforter around my shoulders. Lydia lowers herself into the rocking chair. She leans forward, sympathy etched into her face. Sympathy, and something else.

"Sylvia, I have some . . . news for you. An acquaintance of yours has been in an accident. It was on TV."

"Scott," I say. She raises her eyebrows. "How did you know?"

"He, uh . . . wasn't at school today."

"They found him at the bottom of Lookout Point. He's in stable condition, but he's comatose." She seems to scrutinize my face closely to judge my reaction to this news.

"Well, at least he's alive," I say.

Lydia clears her throat. "You know, Mattie told me what Scott did to you last year. I understand that you must be experiencing some conflicted feelings right now. I want you to know that it's okay if you're not devastated by this news."

I gasp.

"Mattie told you that?"

I can't believe this. Mattie divulged my most guarded secret to a woman who robbed our mother and skipped town twenty years ago, a woman who—it seems—has been screwing with my head ever since she got into town. How could she?

"I didn't want him to get hurt!" I scream. "Get out of my room!"

"We'll get through this together, hon. We really will, okay?"

"Get out!"

Lydia slowly rises and goes to the door. There, she lingers, and she can't resist one last comment. "Don't worry, Sylvia. I'll do whatever I can to protect you girls." And then she's gone.

CHAPTER NINETEEN

I'm in a strange place.

It's dark and raining, and tombstones jut out of the ground all around me.

The cemetery.

For a brief moment, I wonder if I've slid into someone, but when I look down and see my fraying purple robe and fuzzy slippers, I realize I've been hijacked once again.

My first thought is that Lydia is messing with me again, but then I remember I got the picture back from her. I suppose she could have found something else with my imprint on it.

I look down at the grave before me and see my mother's name etched into the stone. I trace my shivering fingers over the cold, hard rock.

SUSAN BELL

Tears spill down my cheeks, mixing with the rain. I fall to the ground and press my face against the grass. If only she were here. She would know what to do. She'd help me untangle the mess with Scotch and clear up the mystery surrounding Aunt Lydia.

"Mom," I say hoarsely. My voice becomes louder, turns into a yell. "Mom!" I'm screaming into the wind. It's a useless noise, my fury against the forces of nature. "Mom! Mom!"

The storm begins to pick up. Lightning spears its way across the sky, and a split second later, thunder slams into my ears. That was close. Too close. But I wonder, maybe it's a sign. Is she listening to me?

I make myself stand up, and the wind pushes me off balance. It knocks me onto the ground. Mud soaks my clothes, and I start to shiver. For a minute, I just lie there, weeping.

Strong arms encircle me. I smell the familiar scent of Rollins's leather jacket. Heat from his body pours through my soaked robe and T-shirt and shorts. He's stroking my hair and whispering to me, but they are angry whispers, full of admonishment.

"What the hell do you think you're doing out here?" he demands.

"What are *you* doing here?" I ask.

"I was driving home from the radio station. I saw some crazy girl walking along the road in her pajamas. Took me a minute to figure out it was you. Vee, you had me scared to death. You must be freezing."

He presses his body against me to warm me up.

Something happens to me in the cemetery.

I become brave.

Beneath Rollins's jacket, I let my fingers explore the places I've never touched before. The muscles on his chest, his back. I nestle my head in the crook of his neck, and we lay there for a second. It just feels right. His hands in my hair, my fingers gliding over the plains and valleys of him.

Panting, I knot my fingers in his hair, pulling him down until his mouth is on my own. For a moment, he hesitates, but then his mouth opens up, and his tongue caresses mine. We writhe against each other, both admitting we need the other in a way we never have before. When thunder crashes around us again, Rollins pulls away. I'm out of breath.

And then I realize.

"Wait. What about Anna?"

Rollins gives me an odd look. "What about her?"

"You've been spending so much time with her. I thought you . . ." I let my words dangle.

He stares at me in amusement. "Vee, the reason I've been spending so much time with her is because you keep pushing me away. I don't like her that way."

I shake my head. "But . . . but the other night, when I tried to kiss you . . . and then someone called, and you rushed out."

He traces my lips with the tip of his finger. "I was preoccupied. My mother fell out of her wheelchair last week and broke her hip. My uncle called, needing help at home."

"Oh," I say, feeling monumentally stupid.

He kisses me again.

Lightning flashes, and a resounding clap from the sky breaks us apart.

"We have to go," Rollins says, and I nod. I let him pull me to my feet and lead me out of the cemetery, weaving our way through the tombstones. We climb the crest of a hill, and I see his car waiting for us in the parking lot.

Inside, Rollins cranks up the heater. "So explain to me what you were doing in the cemetery just now? Let me guess. You don't know how you got there."

I shake my head. "I don't know. I don't remember leaving the house." I pause, thinking of Lydia. Did she purposely lead me to my mother's grave? If she *was* the one to bring me here, what was the point?

If it wasn't Lydia, who was it?

I think of the strange woman who drove me home the night of the accident. Diane. Didn't I see her lurking around my neighborhood again? Could she have something to do with this?

"I don't want to go home." I bite my lip, not knowing where Rollins could take me instead. I've still never been to his house because he's so self-conscious about his incapacitated mother.

"Then come home with me," he says, to my surprise. He shifts his eyes away from the road long enough to look at me and smile shyly. I reach over and grab his hand and squeeze it.

We are silent the rest of the way.

———

When we pull up to his trailer, it is dark with only the flickering light of a television coming from within. I follow him up the crumbling cement path and climb the steps. Rollins shuts the door quietly behind me, and I turn to survey the scene.

A skinny man sits on a raggedy old couch with his feet up on a milk crate that's been repurposed as a coffee table. He's watching Nick@Nite. He looks from the television to Rollins to me, and then returns to his show, taking a swig of his Budweiser.

Rollins leads me toward the back of the trailer. He nods at a door, saying, "My mother's asleep." We continue to the next room, which I recognize instantly as Rollins's. The makeshift bookcase, the jeans slung over the back of a chair, the tattered Stephen King novel lying on his bed. It is so very Rollins.

"Sorry about my uncle," he says. "He'll be leaving for the hospital soon. He always has to psych himself up with a few beers before he goes and cleans up vomit and crap all night. Or at least that's what he says." Vaguely, I remember Rollins telling me his uncle works as a custodian at the hospital.

I sit down on the bed, and he disappears into the hallway, returning a moment later with a faded orange towel. I dab my face and hair dry, but no amount of patting with a little towel is going to dry off my clothes. Pulling off the robe, I realize my white T-shirt has become completely transparent. I feel my face go red as I cross my arms over my chest.

Rollins must have noticed, too, because he looks away, a tiny smile tugging at the corners of his mouth. He pulls open a chipped drawer and finds a Sonic Youth T-shirt to pass my way. From another drawer, he grabs a pair of athletic shorts. I take them gratefully.

"I'm going to duck in the shower," he says. "Be right back."

Once the door closes, I strip off my wet T-shirt and shorts. My whole body is covered in goosebumps. I rub the towel over my skin until I'm reasonably dry and then throw on Rollins's T-shirt and shorts. Then, shivering, I jump into his bed and pull the comforter up to my chin. It takes several minutes for my teeth to stop chattering.

There's a soft rap at the door, and Rollins opens it just wide enough to whisper, "Are you decent?"

"I'm dressed," I say. "The decent thing is debatable."

He laughs and opens the door the rest of the way. I suck in my breath when I see that he's dressed in only a light blue towel, which is knotted around his waist. He goes to his chest of drawers and starts to search for some clothes. I watch the muscles in his back move under his skin. Never have I realized how built Rollins is. I guess he'd have to be, to lift his mother out of her wheelchair all the time.

Rollins slides on some shorts beneath his towel and then pulls on a plain black T-shirt. "My uncle went to work," he says, jutting his thumb in the direction of the living room. "I'll be on the couch if you need anything."

I open my mouth and then—not sure what to say— close it again. I guess I thought he'd sleep in here with me. If not in the bed, then on the floor or something. The thought of sleeping here, by myself, freaks me out. Rollins flips off the light and shuts the door before I can protest.

Turning onto my side, I stare at the sliver of light beneath the door. It's okay. He's only in the next room. I snuggle up in his blankets and breathe in the scent of him. Leather and spice. And something else—something indescribable. Something so Rollins. Like the essence of him.

Seconds pass.

Minutes.

I realize there's no way I'm going to sleep after everything that's happened. My life is such a mess. Someone keeps sliding into me and manipulating me into doing strange things and going weird places. If the police keep searching, they're going to nail me for a crime I didn't commit. I could be put in prison. And now I'm realizing I'm in love with my best friend.

I peel back the covers and slip out of Rollins's bed. Not wanting to wake his mother, I tiptoe across the room and carefully twist the doorknob. The door eases open, and I hurry through the hallway and into the room where Rollins's uncle was watching television only an hour ago.

"Rollins," I whisper.

The lump on the sofa shifts. Rollins opens one eye.

"You okay, Vee? You need some water or something?"

I go to the side of the couch and kneel beside him. "Rollins, can you come back to your room? Please? I can't sleep."

He sits up and yawns.

"Sure. I just didn't want you to be uncomfortable."

"I know," I say, smiling. "But I'd be a lot more comfortable with you there."

Rollins stands, his blanket around his shoulders. I retrace my steps back to his room and wait for him to follow me. I close the door behind us. He starts to arrange the blanket on the floor, but I put my hand on his wrist to stop him.

"No. I want you to sleep with me."

His gaze is steady. "Are you sure?"

I nod.

I climb into bed first, and then he tucks himself in beside me. Though I feel like I know Rollins better than almost anyone in the world, I feel like there's so much history I don't know about. What was his life like before he came to Iowa? Who is his father? What happened to his mother to put her into a wheelchair?

Resting my head on his shoulder, I say, "Tell me about your mom."

He is quiet, and I'm afraid I've pushed too far. Rollins is so protective of his mother. I know he doesn't like to talk about her.

"She had me when she was a teenager," Rollins says. "I never met my dad. He was a drug addict who dumped my mom when he found out she was pregnant. So we lived with my grandparents. My mom worked nights doing custodial work, and when I was big enough to go to school, she got a job with this telemarketing firm. Of course, this was before the accident."

I feel him tense up.

The accident.

"She was riding her bike home from work. She didn't see the car, and the driver didn't see her. At least that's what he said. It was bad. I thought she was going to die. In fact, I remember holding her hand in the hospital, trying not to let her see how scared I was. I was eight years old."

His fingers have gone limp. I knead them, trying to make them come back to life.

"My grandparents took care of her as long as they could. Bathed her. Fed her. But then my grandmother passed away during my freshman year. She died of a heart attack. And my grandfather died soon after, like he didn't have any reason to live anymore. Then it was just me and my mom. My uncle's my only other relative. So we came here. And you . . . you saw the rest."

I think of that day I slid into Rollins, how his uncle screamed at him to give his mother a bath. How gently Rollins undressed her, washed her. It was an act of pure love.

"I'm so sorry," I whisper, pushing a lock of hair out of his eyes.

He shrugs. "You should know better than anyone else. Life isn't always fair."

I turn his face toward mine. His eyes are dark as night. The metal of his lip ring gleams in the moonlight. Running my hands through his hair, I lean in and touch my lips to his. He follows my movements, opening his mouth and letting his tongue caress mine gently.

Before I'm ready for the kiss to be over, Rollins pulls back. "Your turn."

"My turn for what?" I ask, snuggling close to him, trying to entice him into a longer make-out session. But he pulls back and looks at me with serious eyes.

"Your turn to come clean about what's going on. I'm not stupid, Vee."

Every ounce of desire drains out of me as I remember last night, how Scotch's body looked, crumpled and broken. At least he's still alive. At least there's that.

I look at Rollins and realize I can't keep secrets from him any longer. I'm overcome with an urge to tell him everything.

So I do. I describe our plan to teach Scotch a lesson. Then I explain how it went wrong and I'm terrified the police are going to find out that we were there when Scotch fell.

"I didn't see it happen. Someone slid into me right before. I'm afraid whoever it was pushed Scotch."

Rollins doesn't say anything for a moment, and I'm terrified about what he thinks of me. Who lures a guy out into the woods in the middle of the night and leaves him alone and bleeding and maybe even dead? What if Rollins doesn't believe me and thinks I'm making up the story about someone sliding into me to cover up the fact that I pushed him myself?

"Maybe he just fell," he says reassuringly, smoothing my hair.

"There's more. I found something in Lydia's room. The picture of my mother, the one I thought I lost. It was on her bureau. She says she just found it, but I'm not sure I believe her. What if she was using it to slide into me?"

Rollins freezes, his fingers tangled in my hair.

"Shit. That does sound suspicious."

I push myself up on my elbow to get a better look at his face. "So you believe me? I don't sound crazy?"

"Well, the whole situation is messed up. And your aunt sounds psycho. But, no, I don't think you're crazy." I look into his eyes and see that he's telling the truth.

"Will you help me figure out what's going on?"

"Of course I will."

I'm so grateful that Rollins doesn't think I'm insane that I practically pounce on him, nuzzling his neck and earlobe and then his mouth. He grabs me around the waist and flips me onto the bed, hovering above me.

"What are you waiting for?" I ask.

"No more waiting," he says, and then he leans down for a long, warm kiss.

CHAPTER TWENTY

It's five in the morning, and Rollins has parked his car in our driveway. I stare at the house, dreading going inside. Ever since I found out that Lydia had my mother's picture, I feel like I'm starring in some freaky reality show. If she has the power to slide, she could pop in at any moment and observe me. It's beyond unsettling.

"I don't want to go in," I moan.

Rollins squeezes my hand. "You'd better, if you want to be there when everyone wakes up. I'll be back around seven forty-five to pick you up for school."

Almost three hours. I can go back to sleep for a bit, then shower, grab a Pop-Tart, and it'll be time to leave again. That's doable, isn't it? I might not even see Lydia.

"Okay," I say, "but not a second later, promise?"

"I'll be here."

Shyly, I lean in for a kiss. It's funny how quickly things can change. Last fall, if you had asked me how I felt about Rollins, I would have said he was like my brother. I would have been somewhat lying, of course. Every once in a while there'd be a little spark between us, but we were both too chicken to do anything about it. But now. Now, when I press my lips against his, it's like I can't get enough. I don't want him to leave, not even for a second, but I know it's for the best. My dad will freak if he wakes up and I'm gone.

"See you soon," Rollins says softly.

I unbuckle my seat belt and open the door. The air is brisk, and the earth as I cross the lawn is muddy from the storm the night before. My slippers sink with every step.

All seems quiet when I open the door. But when I cross the foyer to tiptoe up the stairs, a voice startles me.

"It's about time."

I turn to see my father and Aunt Lydia sitting at the dining room table, each with a mug of coffee. My father has dark circles beneath his eyes, and I know with sudden certainty that he didn't sleep last night—just like I am positive that I am in deep shit.

Defeated, I slump into the dining room and fall into one of the chairs, avoiding eye contact with both of them. How can I explain my whereabouts last night? Especially when the woman who might have been responsible for my disappearance is sitting right here?

"A little past your curfew, young lady," my father says.

"I don't have a curfew," I say.

"Well, if you did, it certainly wouldn't be five o'clock in the morning," my father says, his voice rising to a near-shout. I notice Lydia discreetly reach out and touch his arm, and he immediately becomes subdued. The intimate gesture infuriates me.

148

"It happened again," I say, looking straight at Lydia, a challenge in my eyes. "I blacked out, and when I woke up, I found myself in the cemetery in the middle of a thunderstorm. Rollins happened to be driving by, and he rescued me."

While my father takes this in, I stare at Lydia, although I'm not exactly sure what I'm looking for. Shame? If she was the one who trotted me out to the cemetery and abandoned me there during a rainstorm, would she look guilty about it? Do I detect a slight wince to reveal her involvement?

I can't be sure, but I think she leans back just slightly, as if my revelation impacted her physically. She looks away from me and then, maybe to cover her reaction, lifts her cup and takes a long sip.

"Rollins just happened to be driving by, huh?" my father says. "Forgive me, Vee, but I'm not sure I buy that."

I shrug. "Buy it or not, that's what happened. I didn't want to wake everyone up, so I just crashed at his place."

My dad shakes his head. "You know, I've always liked Rollins, but this is the second time in two weeks you've been out until all hours of the night."

I look at Lydia. She won't meet my eyes. "I'm sorry, Sylvia. I think your father has a right to know what you've been up to."

My father lets out an exasperated sigh. "Vee, I've always thought of you as the responsible one. Now you're lying to me, not coming home at night. What's next? Are you drinking? Doing drugs?"

"It's not what you think, Dad," I say, but it's no use.

He's already going on, deaf to my protests. "The only solution, I think, is to ground you. If I have to keep you here to make sure you're safe, so be it."

"But—"

"No buts, young lady. You should have thought of that before you betrayed my trust. I'm beginning to think Rollins is a bad influence on you. I want you to take a break from him. I have to work, but Lydia can drive you to school and pick you up. Is that all right with you, Lydia?"

Lydia shoots me a look that is almost remorseful. If I didn't know better, I'd think she actually regretted tattling on me. But she turns to my father and says, "Yes, of course. It's the least I can do."

"It's all set then," my father says, rising from his chair. "I have to get dressed."

"Are you sure you can't call in sick?" Lydia asks. "You've been up all night."

My father tilts his head back, clearly exhausted. "I can't cancel surgery just because my teenage daughter decided to stay out all night with her boyfriend." His words sting like a slap. I feel guilty for making him worry when he has life-and-death matters to be thinking about, but then I remember this isn't *entirely* my fault. Someone slid into me and led me to my mother's grave last night.

I glare at Lydia.

My father walks slowly up the stairs.

"How could you?" I ask when he's out of earshot.

Lydia's brows knit together, and she reaches out as if

to grab my hand across the table. I snatch it away. "I told you, Sylvia. I was your age once. I know what it's like. Sometimes you have to let the older, wiser ones make decisions for you. Don't worry. Your punishment won't last forever. Perhaps I can speak with your father, soften him up a bit . . ."

I stand up quickly, knocking my chair onto the floor. The implication that she is close enough with my father to convince him to lessen my sentence enrages me. What exactly have they been up to when Mattie and I haven't been around? Is it that easy for her to forget the fiancé she left behind in California?

"Don't do me any favors," I mumble, picking up the chair and setting it right. Trembling, I head upstairs, determined to take a long, hot shower and wash away the mental image of Lydia "softening my father up."

Just as I'm texting Rollins to tell him not to bother coming by and that I'll talk to him at school, there's a knock on my door. I pause, thinking it might be Lydia, but then Mattie's muffled voice says, "It's me." I let her inside and close the door behind her, not wanting Lydia to pass by and eavesdrop on our conversation.

Remembering that Mattie shared my private business with Lydia, I cross my arms over my chest. "What exactly did you tell Lydia about Scotch?"

Mattie looks unsure. "Just . . . what happened at the dance. We were looking at an old yearbook, and I was telling her about everyone at school. When we came to a picture of

Scotch, I got kind of quiet. She knew there was something off about him. She kept asking until I told her. Vee, she was furious about what he did to you. Her face got all pale, and she kept clenching her fists. She cares about you."

"I can't believe you told her about that," I say.

"I—I didn't think you'd be so upset," Mattie responds. "I know you don't like Lydia, but I really think she could help us if we told her what happened."

The irony is astounding. Mattie thinks that Lydia can get us out of a mess that, in all probability, she created.

"Look," I say after taking a deep breath. "Don't tell her anything more. Just give me today to think about what we should do."

Mattie nods after a moment. "I heard Scotch is still alive. That's good, right?"

"Yeah, it's good. Except when he wakes up, he'll probably tell everyone he was with Regina before he fell. And then she'll crumble and spill everything."

Mattie's face clouds, as if she hadn't thought of this complication. She crosses the room and sits on the bed, letting her head fall into her hands.

She looks so miserable that I regret yelling at her. I sit down next to her and rub her back. "Don't worry. I'll fix everything."

I don't know how.

But I will.

On the way to school, I stare out the window of Lydia's lemon-yellow Toyota. Mattie is in the front, and I am in the back, trying to ignore the way Lydia keeps attempting to make eye contact with me in the rearview mirror.

"So, guys, isn't prom coming up pretty soon?" Lydia asks, flipping the radio dial until she finds some cheesy pop station. She sways her head with the beat.

I roll my eyes.

"Yep," Mattie says. "In a couple of weeks."

"Has anyone asked you yet?" Lydia puts on her turn signal and drives past McDonald's. She directs the question to Mattie, probably realizing that it wouldn't matter if Johnny freaking Depp asked me, because I'm grounded.

"No, but there is this guy I've been talking to. Russ. He's a senior, but he's actually Vee's age. We're supposed to go to the movies with Rollins and Vee on Friday."

I can sense Lydia throwing a questioning look in my direction, but I don't give her the satisfaction of meeting her gaze. "Really?" she finally says.

"Yeah," Mattie replies. "Hey, Vee, did you ask Dad about that yet?"

I clench my teeth. "Not yet."

Lydia pulls into the school parking lot and shifts the car into park.

"Thanks for the ride, Lydia. I've got practice after school, so I'll probably just catch a ride with Samantha or someone."

"All right. Have a good day, honey." Lydia calling Mattie *honey* strikes me as ingenuous, the way a salesgirl at a department store might address you when goading you into trying on some expensive perfume. But Mattie doesn't seem to notice. She just waves and slams the door.

I make a move to exit the vehicle, but Lydia turns around to face me. "Wait a second, Vee. I want to talk to you."

"What?"

"I don't want you to hate me," she says.

"Um, then why did you get me grounded?"

A silence hangs between us for a moment, and it seems that she's on the verge of confessing something. My breath quickens, and I wonder if she's about to reveal her sliding ability. But then her face changes, and I know she's not going to come clean.

"Everything I'm doing is for your own good. I wish you'd believe that."

"Okay, I believe it. Now let me go to school. I'm going to be late for first period."

She nods. "Okay," she says weakly. "I'll be here at three thirty."

Without another word, I scramble out of the car and slam the door behind me.

CHAPTER TWENTY-ONE

I'm yanking books out of my backpack and throwing them into my locker when someone taps on my shoulder. I turn to find Rollins, his eyebrows raised. "So what's up?"

"I got busted. My dad thinks I basically snuck out to spend the night with you."

"Didn't you tell him what happened?"

"Yeah, but he doesn't believe me. Lydia told him that I was also out of the house on Thursday night, so he *grounded* me. Lydia's supposed to be driving me to and from school from now on."

"You're kidding."

"I wish," I say, grabbing my English notebook.

"Well, at least we can still see each other at school. Lunchtime? Under the bleachers?" Rollins murmurs, leaning close. I close my eyes, feeling his warmth so close to me. His lips press against mine, and all the bad things seem to melt away, if only for a moment.

When I open my eyes, I'm greeted with a decidedly unwelcome sight.

Anna.

"Oh, I'm sorry, guys. Rollins, I just wanted to make sure we're still on for this afternoon."

I raise my eyebrows at Rollins, who scratches the back of his head.

"You know, you were going to help me with my play-list?"

"Oh. Oh, yeah, Anna. I totally forgot. But I think I'm free after school. That shouldn't be a problem." He looks at me questioningly.

"Well, don't let me stop you. I'll be at home, counting the daisies on the wallpaper in the kitchen."

"Great. I mean, not great. . . . You know what I mean," Rollins says, flustered. "See you at lunch?"

I sigh. "Sure."

I watch Rollins walk off down the hallway with Anna, noticing how her vintage jeans hug her butt so perfectly. It's how magazines say your butt should look, like an apple or an upside-down heart or something stupid like that. I can't help comparing it with my own straight-as-a-board ass.

I try to comfort myself by remembering what Rollins said to me last night.

I don't like her that way.

But it's not enough to quell the uneasiness I feel when I see Anna reach over and grab Rollins's arm. And he doesn't pull away.

Mrs. Winger spends the first ten minutes of class reviewing vocabulary on the projector. I try to follow along, but I keep finding myself staring at the clock, counting the minutes until lunch. Once or twice, I try to catch Samantha's eye, but she purposely looks away every time.

Mrs. Winger turns off the projector. "Okay, go ahead and put away your notes. I'd like you to get together with the partners you were with yesterday when we read 'Young Goodman Brown.' Today I want you to come up with a practice thesis for a literary analysis paper. Whenever you're ready, you may go sit with your partner."

I gather my books and move them to the desk next to Samantha's. She ignores me, taking out a fresh piece of notebook paper and smoothing it on her desk.

When everyone seems to be absorbed in their work, I say, under my breath, "I told."

Samantha writes our names at the top of the paper. After a minute, she says, just as quietly, "I kind of figured that out. I saw a bunch of cops in the office this morning."

My voice is urgent. "You know I had to."

Samantha shakes her head disgustedly.

At that moment, the door opens, and Officer Teahen steps inside. Samantha's eyes widen, and then she drops her head down. Officer Teahen walks over to Mrs. Winger and speaks to her quietly. She goes to her desk, shuffles through some papers, finds what she's looking for, and hands it to the police officer. As she gives it to him, the paper tilts just enough for me to see that it's a class list.

"Melissa Abraham," Officer Teahen says, and the girl whose name he just called eyes him nervously. "Could you come with me for just a second?"

Melissa stands, looking at Mrs. Winger questioningly. The plump English teacher nods, as if to tell her to go ahead. Officer Teahen politely waits for Melissa to make her way to the front of the room, and then he follows her into the hallway, closing the door with a soft click.

Samantha and I look at each other.

You're next, she mouths, and for a second I have no idea what she's talking about. Then it hits me. Officer Teahen is calling on students alphabetically. Technically, Billy Armstrong should be next in line for questioning, but the cops aren't looking for guys. The person who made the 911 call was a female. When Officer Teahen returns with Melissa Abraham, he'll call the next girl on the list.

Sylvia Bell.

Me.

I swallow.

My palms start to sweat. I can't imagine looking into Officer Teahen's eyes and explaining my plan to him, the plan to teach Scotch Becker a lesson, the plan that resulted in a catastrophic fall that could have led to his death. That probably *would* have led to his death if I'd waited any longer to make that 911 call.

Guilt is a funny feeling. You can evade it for a while, but it always creeps back. I tried to convince myself that I'd done nothing wrong, that Scotch's fall was the fault of Lydia or whoever slid into me that night. But when it comes right down to it, the whole thing was my idea. If not for me, Scotch would be at school right now, making lewd jokes about the lunch ladies.

And now that it's time for me to spill everything that I know, I'm not ready. I feel like wrenching open one of the windows and running away before my name can be called. I feel like, at the very least, asking to go to the girls' room and hanging out there for the rest of the period.

And then it dawns on me.

I have the perfect excuse.

Because of my so-called narcolepsy, I have a permanent hall pass. Whenever I start to feel woozy, I can ask my teachers to let me go to the nurse, and they have to say yes. They don't want me to collapse in their classrooms.

I push myself into a standing position and walk up to Mrs. Winger. "Is it okay if I go to the nurse?" I ask.

Her eyes flick up to me.

She sighs.

"Sure, Sylvia."

I pick up the hall pass from Mrs. Winger's desk on my way out. As I go by Melissa Abraham's desk, I scan her belongings quickly. Did she leave anything behind that's personal enough to carry an emotional charge? There's an open notebook with a few sentences about "Young Goodman Brown." A slightly chewed-up pencil. A half-full bottle of water.

My eyes drop lower, to her purse, which is propped up against her chair. There's a little silver key chain in the shape of a heart hanging off the strap—the kind of thing a girl's parents or her boyfriend might give her for Christmas or her birthday.

Bingo.

I pretend to trip and drop the hall pass onto the ground.

"Oops," I mumble.

A few kids look my way, but their eyes promptly return to the doorway. Everyone is curious about what the policeman is doing at our school. I take advantage of the distraction to shoot my hand out and unclasp the key chain from Melissa's purse. I stuff it into my pocket and straighten up. No one looks in my direction. On my way out of the room, I pray that Melissa doesn't return before I do. It might be awkward, trying to explain why I have her key chain.

The hallway is empty. I turn right and make a beeline for the only place I know I won't be disturbed—the staff restroom. While the girls' room has multiple stalls, this bathroom only has one toilet and the ability to lock the door. They even have a cushy chair in the corner of the room, next to a dusty plastic plant and an end table. I'm not sure why anyone would want to hang out in there, but whatever.

After one last look to make sure no one is around to see me duck into the staff bathroom, I push my way inside and twist the lock behind me.

In two seconds flat, I fish Melissa's key chain out of my pocket and throw myself into the chair. Squeezing my eyes closed, I hold the trinket in the palm of my hand and wait.

And wait.

And wait.

My heart is pounding too hard, I realize. I'm amped up with so much adrenaline, there's no way I'll be able to slide. I try to make myself relax by taking deep breaths and clearing my mind, but I keep seeing Scotch's body at the bottom of the cliff.

Behave, I tell my brain angrily, but that's the thing about brains. They never do what you want them to do, especially if you're trying *not* to think about something. The more I struggle to empty my mind, the clearer the picture of Scotch's twisted figure becomes.

I open my eyes and heave a sigh of frustration.

Let's face it. It's not going to work.

When I open the door, I see Officer Teahen and Melissa coming my way. I turn around quickly and walk back toward the classroom.

I can hear them talking behind me.

"So you say Scotch was hanging out with Samantha Phillips last week? Were they dating? Do you think he would have gone to Lookout Point with her?"

Melissa's voice is squeaky. "Maybe. I wouldn't put it past her. She's in Mrs. Winger's class right now if you want to talk to her."

Officer Teahen says, "I just might do that."

I walk a little faster.

Back in the room, I slip into my seat next to Samantha and lean over. My voice is barely above a whisper. "I heard the cop talking to Melissa in the hall. She told him you went to the party with Scotch last week. He wants to talk to you next."

"Oh, great," Samantha murmurs.

The door opens, and Melissa comes in. She avoids eye contact with Samantha and returns to her desk. Officer Teahen walks swiftly to Mrs. Winger's desk and says something in a low voice. She gestures toward Samantha, and his eyes follow.

"Samantha?" Mrs. Winger says. "Could you come up here for a second?"

Samantha stands up and walks over to Mrs. Winger's desk, throwing me a dark look over her shoulder. I watch as she listens to Officer Teahen, nods, and then follows him out of the room.

The rest of the class seems to last forever. I stare at Samantha's notebook, in which she's made several unintelligible notes about "Young Goodman Brown." I doodle in the margins, counting the seconds.

After an eternity, the bell rings. Everyone gathers up their things and heads for the door. I hear more than one person speculating about why the cop was taking such a long time with Samantha.

A sudden cry pulls me away from my thoughts.

It's Melissa Abraham. She is holding her purse in front of her, panic on her face. "Mrs. Winger! Mrs. Winger!"

Mrs. Winger rushes over. "What is it, Melissa?"

"Someone stole my key chain."

Shit.

"What? Are you sure? It probably just fell off. What

does it look like?" Mrs. Winger stoops down and scans the carpet.

"It's a little heart. Actually, it's my sister's, but she let me borrow it. She'll kill me if she found out I lost it."

I discreetly pull the key chain out and flick it onto the carpet several feet away from me. Mrs. Winger continues her inspection, inching her way in my direction.

"Is that it?" I ask, pointing to the key chain.

Melissa hurries over. "Ohmigod, thank you *so much* for finding it." She bends over and scoops it up.

"No problem," I say, feeling a twinge of guilt. "It's very pretty."

"Thanks," Melissa replies. "See you around."

Mrs. Winger gives me a grateful smile and then looks down at Samantha's desk. "Oh, dear. Samantha isn't back yet. Will you see her later today? Would you mind gathering her things?"

"No problem," I repeat, but in my head I'm thinking that's a lie.

I do have a problem.

A huge freaking problem.

CHAPTER TWENTY-TWO

In the hall, I spot Samantha stalking my way.

"This is all your fault," she says.

"Shhhh," I say. "Let's go somewhere more private." I grab her arm, but she shakes me off and heads toward the bathroom. I follow her, cringing. Once inside, I hold out the stack of notebooks she left behind in Mrs. Winger's room. "Here are your things."

Samantha snatches the pile of books and slams them onto a sink. A freshman girl comes out of one of the stalls, and Samantha gives her a look scornful enough to make the poor girl scurry out of the room without washing her hands.

After the door swings closed, Samantha begins whispering angrily. "So that cop totally thinks I pushed Scotch."

"Did he say that?" I say, my heart sinking.

"No, but what else is he supposed to think? Scotch drove me home from the party on Thursday night. If he asks around, he's sure to find out that Scotch spread those nasty rumors about me. It's the only logical conclusion."

I shake my head. "I don't think that's enough to pin Scotch's fall on you. He'd need evidence that you were there that night. A witness, or something."

Samantha stares stonily at me. "And what do you think Regina's going to say when she's called in for questioning?"

I lift my hands to my temples and try to rub away the headache that is steadily building. There's only one way to fix this. I have to confess. "Samantha, I'll talk to the cops. I'll explain what happened. We didn't mean—"

Samantha grabs my shoulders and shakes me. "No! All you were doing was trying to help me. I'll be damned if you get in trouble for this. We'll talk to Regina. I'll make sure she doesn't say anything. We have to stick together. Okay?"

I remember how Mattie begged me to stay quiet.

"Okay," I say finally. "Okay."

There's something disturbing about watching Rollins crack up at Anna's jokes. Even though I know they're just friends. Even though I trust him completely. It's like a tornado of jealousy inside me when I watch them together. Especially when Rollins and I are supposed to be alone right now. Instead, he brought Anna to eat lunch with us under the bleachers.

This is *our* spot. It may be littered with decaying leaves and candy-bar wrappers, but it's *ours*. And now he's desecrating it with Anna and her joke about Mrs. Winger and her addiction to computer solitaire. She's not even funny.

Miffed, I take a giant bite of my Pop-Tart.

"So I've been thinking about my playlist for tonight," Anna says, giving Rollins a serious look. "I want a nice mix of old and new, like something really cool. A little Emily's Army mixed with some Nina Simone, maybe."

Rollins looks thoughtful. "Totally agree. You just want to make sure it segues smoothly. I've got some ideas for you."

She brightens. "Great!"

I cough. Rollins looks at me as though he forgot I was here. "Oh, shit, Vee. This has to be so boring for you. I'm sorry."

Haughtily, I say, "I'm interested in music. Maybe I've got ideas, too."

They both stare at me, waiting for me to go on.

I panic, trying to think of something cool to say. I see a kid in a tie-dye T-shirt walking into school. "How about some Jimi Hendrix?"

Anna blinks, and Rollins rubs my shoulder. "I don't think that's exactly the type of playlist Anna had in mind, Vee. She's focusing on female artists, anyway."

"Oh," I say, popping the last bit of Pop-Tart into my mouth and standing up—well, standing up the best I can underneath the bleachers. Really, I'm more crouching than anything. "I'm done. I'll leave you two to finish your discussion."

Rollins looks from me to Anna. "Wait. Don't go. We can talk about this later."

"No, it's fine," I say, already shuffling away, kicking leaves as I go. "I'll see you in Intro to Psych."

I expect him to come after me. I mean, I know it's pretty childish of me, but I really do. The fact that he *doesn't* kind of rips me up inside. I stand outside the school, counting to a hundred, but he never comes.

So I go inside alone.

Between classes, Mattie catches my arm and pulls me into an empty doorway. Her face is serious. Immediately, I imagine the worst. Did Officer Teahen already question her? Are we all going to jail for our idiotic prank?

"What is it?"

Mattie looks around cautiously and speaks in a low voice. "Regina texted me. She's not at school today. She went to visit Scotch at the hospital."

My stomach drops. "He's awake?"

"No, but she's convinced she'll be able to get him to wake up if she sits and talks to him."

For a moment, I'm ashamed of myself for feeling relieved that Scotch hasn't awakened. As long as he's asleep, he's quiet, making my life so much easier.

"Okay," I say, trying to figure out what this means for us. "Okay."

If Regina is visiting Scotch at the hospital, it's only a matter of time before it comes out that she's the one who was with him that night. And when the cops find her, she'll lead them to us. Samantha is going to freak when she finds out where Regina is.

"Shit," I finally say. "This isn't good. Were his parents there?"

"No. She told the nurse she was his sister. I think she feels guilty for what happened. She keeps talking about what a tough life Scotch has. How she wants to be there for him."

My mind is racing. "We've got to get her out of there before Scotch's parents—or worse, the cops—show up."

Someone touches my arm. Rollins.

"What's wrong?"

"Rollins, could you give me a ride to the hospital? Regina's there, visiting Scotch. I'm afraid she's going to say something stupid."

Rollins nods. "Sure. I didn't really feel like going to Psych today anyway."

"Can I come?" Mattie looks at me hopefully.

"No. You stay here. If we get caught, I don't want both of us to get in trouble. Okay?" I put my hand on my sister's shoulder. She nods reluctantly and then heads toward her next class.

I watch my sister sulk away, her cell phone close to her ear. Regret floods through me. She shouldn't have to be dealing with things like this. She should be able to giggle and talk to Russ and daydream about what color her prom dress will be.

I shake my head sadly and follow Rollins toward the exit. As we're ducking out, I see Officer Teahen at the other end of the hallway. My heart pounding, I grab Rollins by the sleeve and pull him out the door.

"What was that all about?" Rollins asks when we're safely inside his car. "You just about yanked my arm off."

I frown. "Officer Teahen is here at school question-ing people. I was going to tell you at lunch, but Anna was there."

Rollins gapes at me. "Holy shit. Did he talk to you?"

I shake my head. "He pulled Samantha out of English. She said she got a ride home from the party with Scotch on Thursday night but didn't tell about our little plot to get back at him. It's only a matter of time, though. If the cops talk to Regina, it would be bad."

Turning the key in the ignition, Rollins says, "Sorry about lunch. Anna kind of ambushed me."

I shrug. "No biggie."

"Really? I got the impression you were a little pissed."

"Well, maybe a little."

We pull out of the school parking lot. I keep my eyes peeled for any policemen, but there's no one.

Rollins reaches over and squeezes my knee. "I'll make it up to you. That's a promise."

The warmth from his fingers radiates upward. It's almost enough to make me forget that Regina is at the hospital right now, about to completely blow our cover.

Almost.

CHAPTER TWENTY-THREE

The intensive care unit is on the fourth floor. I tap my foot, willing the elevator to travel faster.

Second floor.

Third floor.

The doors slide open, and a pretty nurse with red hair pushes a wheelchair into the small space in front of us. She gives us a suspicious look, probably wondering why we're not in school. Or maybe I'm just being paranoid.

My father works on the sixth floor, and I'm banking on the fact that he spends most of his day behind steel doors, carefully working to make sick babies well again.

Finally, we reach the fourth floor. The nurse pulls the wheelchair sideways to let Rollins and me get off the elevator. We walk into a waiting area. There's a desk off to the right side. Beyond that, the hallway that leads to the patients' rooms.

"Wait here," I say.

I've been at the hospital enough times to know that you can go almost anywhere, as long as you act like you have a right to be there. The only place security is really tight is in the maternity ward, where the guards are constantly watching out for baby snatchers.

I give the lady behind the desk a bright smile and start to walk past her, toward the hallway.

"Who do you need to see, sweetie?" she asks.

Crap. Of course I run into the one nurse who follows protocol.

I stop in my tracks. "Hi, um, I'm a friend of Scott Becker's sister. Her phone is off, and I have something urgent to tell her."

The nurse gives me a strange look. "His sister isn't here. She left about twenty minutes ago. His parents are here, though. I can call them for you. . . ." The nurse lifts the phone from its cradle and poises her finger, about to dial a number.

"Oh, no. That's okay. You say she left? I'll go find her."

The nurse frowns at me. Before she can say anything else, I turn on my heel and head toward Rollins.

Go! I mouth at him. He turns back toward the elevator and jabs the down button with his thumb.

"Miss?" I hear the nurse call behind me.

I pretend not to hear.

The elevator doors open up. Rollins and I hop in, and I hurriedly press the button for the lobby. As the doors close, I risk a look back at the desk. The nurse, annoyed that I ignored her, is glaring at me. But there's someone else standing beside her—another nurse, with her hair pulled back into a bun.

My heart races when I recognize who it is.

Diane.

"So *that* was the woman who gave you a ride home after your accident?" Rollins asks, steering his car back toward the school. "Strange that she just happens to be working in the same part of the hospital where Scotch is being kept."

"Yup," I reply. I'm lost in thought, trying to figure out what the hell she was doing there. It doesn't compute. Could it really be a coincidence that I met her the same night I got into an accident, on the same road that Scotch was driving on only minutes before? It just doesn't make any sense.

"It's almost three thirty. Do you want me to just drop you off at home?"

I snap to attention. "What? Crap. Lydia's supposed to pick me up. If she sees us, she'll know I skipped school and will report back to my father. He'll be even madder at you than he already is."

Rollins taps the steering wheel with his fingertips. "I could drop you off at the back entrance. Then you can go in and get your books and come out the front."

"Yeah, let's do that," I say.

Rollins pulls up to the curb at the back of the school. Distracted, I lean over to give him a quick kiss.

"Don't forget to call me tonight," he says.

"I won't," I promise.

I slam the car door shut and hurry into the school.

———

Sure enough, Lydia's yellow car is waiting outside the school for me at three thirty. She's got sunglasses propped up on her forehead, even though the sky is overcast, and I notice she took the time to swipe on some bright red lipstick before leaving the house.

"Hey, honey. How was your day?" she asks when I open the passenger door and scoot inside. She sounds chipper, like she's playing the part of a mother in some sitcom from the fifties. I get this creepy feeling, like a house centipede has curled up on the back of my neck.

"Super," I say. "Another day in paradise."

My sarcastic remark dampens her cheer. She starts the car. "Come on, Vee. I could do with a little less attitude. How can we have any fun together if you're pouting the whole time?"

I stare at her as she pulls out of the parking lot. She doesn't make any sense. First, she swirls into our lives like a hurricane, out of nowhere. Then she spies on me until she finds some dirt. She tries to get on my good side by swearing she won't tell my dad I snuck out of the house. And then she blabs and gets me grounded. For the life of me, I can't figure out what the hell she wants from me.

"Do you mind if we take a detour?" she asks, signaling a turn that would take us downtown.

Something warns me to be careful about where I let this woman take me. After all, what do I know about her? She lied about her fiancé back in California. She was living her life with a false name. I caught her going through my father's drawers. And there's just something about her that gives me the creeps—something about the way she seems so desperate to fit into our family. Still, I can't help but feel curious. Maybe this is my chance to find out more about her.

"Um. Okay?" I say finally.

She gives me a sideways glance and bursts out laughing. "Don't look so freaked out, Vee! I just want to go grab some pie."

She parks in front of a small diner. My dad used to bring us here when we were little, but I haven't eaten here in years. It's one of those faux fifties restaurants with a jukebox and all of the waitresses wearing poodle skirts.

Lydia plugs a few quarters into the meter on the sidewalk, and then I follow her inside. She drums her fingers on the little podium as we wait for someone to seat us, seeming a few degrees more nervous than she did in the car. I wonder exactly what she wants to talk to me about.

A girl a few years older than me sidles up and flashes a big grin. "Hi, ladies. Just the two of you?" I can smell the watermelon from her chewing gum. She looks familiar. Her long, blond hair is swept up into a high ponytail, and her face is fresh with only a dab of pink lip gloss. I realize she played Annie Oakley in the school production of *Annie Get Your Gun* when I was a freshman. Melody, I think her name is.

"Just the two of us," Lydia says brightly.

Melody motions for us to follow her to a booth. She waits for us to get settled and then asks for our drink orders. I order a Coke and look at Lydia, who is sitting across from me, looking blankly at Melody.

"I'm sorry. What did you say?" Lydia asks. She must be planning on bringing up something big if she can't even pay attention to the waitress.

"Would you like something to drink?"

"Just an ice water," Lydia says.

Melody nods and then heads behind the counter to prepare the drinks. I grab one of the menus, staring but not comprehending.

"So there's a reason I brought you here, Vee," Lydia says. Her voice is tight.

"Nostalgia for a golden age?" I ask, not able to look her in the eye now that I'm sitting across from her.

"Nope. That's just a perk. I have something to give you." Lydia plops her purse on the table and starts going through it, searching for something. Finally, she pulls out a red velvet box. I'd recognize it anywhere. It's the box my dad keeps my mom's wedding ring in.

She offers it to me, the fancy box sitting in the palm of her hand. For a minute, all I can do is stare at it. Since my mother died, I've never seen it outside the context of my father's bedroom. This whole situation is surreal.

"Take it," she says.

Shaking, I reach across the table and grab the box out of her hand. I hold it in my lap, enclosed in both hands, as if it might grow wings and fly away from me.

"Aren't you going to look inside?"

"I already know what's inside," I say coldly.

My icy tone doesn't register with her. Melody brings us our drinks, not seeming to notice the tense vibe at our table, and asks what we'd like to eat. Lydia orders a piece of banana cream pie. I say I'm not hungry.

When Melody leaves, Lydia says, "You don't know. Open it."

I force myself to look her in the eye. There is a challenge in her expression. So I muster up the strength and crack the box open and see—

"What the hell?"

A gorgeous necklace is nestled at the bottom of the box. With one hand, I lift the thin silver chain and examine the pendant. Set in the center is a beautiful diamond surrounded by rubies in the shape of a heart. It takes me a minute, but then I realize the diamond is the same one that was in my mother's ring.

"What is this?"

"It's a necklace," she says with a teasing smile.

"Uh, yeah. I see that it's a necklace. Where did you get it?"

"Your father told me he'd been considering having the ring made into a necklace for you. I begged him to let me design it. He's a man. He doesn't know about jewelry. Do you like it?"

I remember the day I found her in my father's bedroom, fingering my mother's ring. Is it possible she was examining it to design this necklace? I honestly don't know what to believe anymore.

"It's beautiful," I say flatly, dropping the necklace back into the box.

"You don't look happy," Lydia observes. "I thought you'd love this."

"Well, you thought wrong," I say, thinking that I really would love the gift, if only my father had given it to me.

Melody sets a piece of banana cream pie before Lydia and returns to the front of the restaurant to wait on a couple of little old ladies.

"I think I know what your problem is," Lydia says, stirring the ice in her water with a straw.

"Oh yeah?" I challenge her.

"Yeah. I think you're mad at me because I dated your father in high school. But you don't have to worry about that. It's ancient history. Any feelings I had for him died long ago."

My mouth falls open.

Lydia dated my *father*?

Does that mean that he was the one my mom and aunt were fighting over? I feel myself getting nauseous.

"Is that why you're angry?" Lydia looks at me expectantly.

"Can I get you guys anything else?" Melody's voice causes me to jump.

"Could we get the check?" I ask.

I have to get out of here.

Now.

When we get home, Lydia says she has a headache and goes upstairs to lie down. I find Mattie sitting at the kitchen table, eating a bowl of cereal.

"Where were you guys?"

"At that old diner Dad used to take us to. Mattie, I have something to tell you about Lydia. Something you're not going to like."

I expect Mattie to look worried or upset. Instead, she takes another bite of her Lucky Charms. "I bet I already know what you're going to say," she says, her mouth full. "Dad dated Lydia in high school, right?"

"How did you know?" I stare at her.

Mattie swallows. "She told me."

"How could you *not* tell me?"

"Um, because I knew you'd freak out? It's really not a big deal. It happened ages and ages ago. Besides, it's not like she still has feelings for him. She has a fiancé back in California."

"You knew about that, too?" I stand up, my cheeks growing warm with anger. Suddenly, I want to tell Mattie something she doesn't know about Lydia. I need to show her that she doesn't know our aunt as well as she thinks she does.

"Did you know that Lydia has been going by a different name in California?"

Mattie looks confused. "What are you talking about?"

"I went through her suitcase one day after school when she was out. I found her wallet. There were credit cards and an ID with the name Lila Harrington on them. I was able to find her fiancé online by Googling her fake name. I called him, and he doesn't even know where she is. If Lydia is as trustworthy as you think, why would she leave her fiancé without telling him where she was going?"

Mattie shakes her head. "She must have a good reason for not being truthful. Maybe he was abusive or something. Maybe she's hiding from him."

I throw my hands up in the air. If Mattie still trusts our aunt, even with the evidence that she's been lying to the people closest to her, I don't know what to say.

"Did she give you the necklace?" Mattie asks.

"I can't believe this. You knew about the necklace too?"

A smile plays upon Mattie's lips. "Isn't it pretty?"

I don't respond. Instead, I stalk out of the kitchen. It kills me, the fact that Mattie and Lydia are acting like besties out of nowhere. Brushing each other's hair. Talking about Mom. Discussing my private business.

Mattie's *my* sister.

I'm supposed to be the one she shares everything with.

And I was.

Until Lydia came along.

CHAPTER TWENTY-FOUR

Later that afternoon, I'm sitting on my bed, staring at the necklace Lydia gave to me in the diner. The sunlight streaming through my window illuminates the diamond, and I can see angles and shapes, deep inside, that I never noticed before. It is so familiar, the stone I saw on my mother's finger whenever she pushed me on a swing or stirred marshmallows into a mug of hot cocoa for me.

I pick up the necklace and hold it before me, swinging like a pendulum. I'm overcome with the need to put it on, to hold that part of my mother close to my heart. My hands shaking, I fasten the clasp around my neck, and then look down. The pendant rests at the hollow of my throat as if it was always meant to be there.

My eyelids start to droop, and I lower myself onto my pillow. These last few days have been exhausting. I allow myself to drift away, and the edges of the room become fuzzy. Then all is black.

I'm standing in our kitchen, rinsing tomatoes in the sink. My hands scrub the dirt from the firm, red fruit. The fingers are long, tipped with pale pink nail polish. I've slid into Lydia. She must have left some emotional residue on the necklace. Maybe she misses my mother more than I realized.

I hear my father's voice, talking about something funny that happened at work today, a story about a nurse whose husband sent her a gift certificate to a nearby gym for their anniversary. He sounds relaxed and happy—the most carefree he's been in months.

"How horrible," Lydia says, but her giggles betray her. She glances up from her work to smile at my father, who takes her laughter as a sign of encouragement and launches into another story.

I should be glad that my father has someone to tell his boring stories to, someone who appreciates them more than Mattie or I do. But I can't help but feel disgusted. Why didn't he tell me the truth about Lydia? Is he starting to have feelings for her again? Do I detect a note of flirtation in his jokes?

When I slide out of the domestic scene, I am immersed in dread. Lydia said she wanted to get to know us better, really be a part of our family. Could she have meant that literally? She's already won over my sister. What if she puts the moves on my father? Is it possible she could be aiming to reclaim his affection?

———

I sit up and look around. My room is just as it was when I fell asleep, the violet walls darkening as the sun dips lower in the sky. The chain around my neck pulls taut, caught on a knot in my hair. I look down in dismay at the necklace. If I wear the necklace, I will always risk sliding into Lydia. It's now tainted.

I reach behind my neck and undo the clasp, pulling the necklace free. Carefully, I return it to the red velvet box and hide it in my bottom drawer, along with Scotch's father's glove and the various other items I've collected that allow me to slide into others.

I go to my mother's rocking chair and sit down, pressing my face against the wood worn smooth over the years. I close my eyes and think of her and my father, how they used to laugh together in the kitchen while they prepared dinner. Now, Lydia is the one making my father smile, and I can't stand it.

My father and Lydia are strangely giddy at dinner. They've each had a couple of glasses of wine, and they keep looking at each other and grinning and then looking away. Their thinly veiled flirtations make my stomach churn.

My father's eyes gleam as he laughs at one of Lydia's stories about her students in California. It must be impossible for him to not see Mom in Lydia when he looks at her. Doesn't he see that it's a betrayal, for him to reconnect with Mom's sister?

Mattie, not seeming to notice the shift in tone between

my father and Lydia, scoops a bite of spaghetti into her mouth. "Mmmm," she says. "This sauce is delicious."

"That would be Lydia's doing," my father says. "She shared a new recipe with me." I think of my mother's cookbook, stashed away, forgotten. What was wrong with *her* recipe?

"Hey, Dad. Did you decide whether I can go to that movie with Russ and Vee and Rollins Saturday night?"

My dad's pleasant expression fades, replaced with confusion. "I'm sorry. Vee and Rollins and *who*?"

Mattie turns her attention to me. "Didn't you talk to him yet? God, you've had forever."

"Talk to me about what?"

"Russ is this guy from school. He's a senior, but he's really only Vee's age. He's just supersmart. He asked me out. I thought it would be okay if we doubled with Vee and Rollins."

Dad crosses his arms. "Well, there's just one problem with that. Vee is grounded."

"What? You didn't tell me that," Mattie says to me. "Why are you grounded?"

I shrug, giving her a pointed look. "*You* don't tell *me* a lot of things."

Lydia jumps in. "It's just a movie, Jared. What kind of trouble can she get in there?" I glare at her. I don't need anyone to stand up for me, especially *her*.

Seeming to forget about my punishment, Mattie continues to nag my father. "Yeah, Dad. We'll be home by midnight. Eleven, even. We'll go to the early show."

Lydia touches my father's arm. "What do you say, Jared?"

He takes another bite of spaghetti. "Fine, fine. Be home by midnight. *Both of you.*" His final words are directed at me.

"Does this mean I can start hanging out with Rollins again?"

My father exchanges a look with Lydia. "I suppose so. As long as you never stay out all night again. Is that clear?"

I nod. Lydia gives me a look like she's done me some big favor. I take a bite of my pasta and make a face, showing what I think of her special recipe.

CHAPTER TWENTY-FIVE

The next morning, I find Lydia making a pot of coffee. I turn on my heel, hoping to avoid conversation, but it's too late. She sees me.

"Good morning, Vee."

Reluctantly, I turn back. "Oh, hey." I grab a banana from the counter and peel it slowly, avoiding eye contact. I'm grateful for being ungrounded, but the fact that she had anything to do with it irritates me to no end.

"Are you ready to go? I just need to grab my purse, and then I'm all set."

I blink. "Rollins is coming to get me. He always gives me a ride, and now that I'm not grounded anymore . . ."

"Oh." She looks disappointed.

I take a bite of my banana and throw the peel in the trash. "Yeah."

Lydia takes a step toward me. "Vee, why are you so hostile toward me?"

I finish chewing and swallow. "It's simple. You disappeared for twenty years and then just showed up and expected us to welcome you with open arms, like nothing ever happened. You want to instantly be part of our family, but you haven't done the legwork. To me, there's something just a little bit creepy about that. Especially now that I know you have a past with my father. Does he know that you go by the name Lila Harrington these days?"

My last words hang in the air between us.

Lydia crosses her arms over her chest. "You went through my things."

There's no point in trying to deny it. "Yeah, I did. You didn't answer my question. Does my father know about your new name? Or that you left a fiancé behind in California?"

"Vee, my past is . . . complicated. I'd rather not discuss these issues with your father, if it's all the same to you.

"Look," I say. "Either you tell my father, or I will."

We are staring at each other when Mattie comes sailing into the room.

"Hey, we needed to leave like ten minutes ago. I'm supposed to retake a Spanish quiz this morning."

Someone honks in the driveway. Rollins. Right on time.

"I've got to run. I'm sure Lydia won't mind giving you a lift."

I walk out of the room, leaving Mattie with her new best friend.

The hallway is filled with the rubbery squeaks from wet sneakers. Even though it's a Friday, everyone seems muted, like they're all actually asleep but just going through the motions. I'm standing with Rollins at his locker, flipping through his iPod while he locates his math book.

Anna appears from out of nowhere. "Hi, Vee."

"Hi," I say curtly.

Rollins straightens up. "Oh, hey, Anna. How's it going?"

"Great. I'm soooo excited to see *Scar IV* tomorrow night."

Rollins flicks his eyes toward me. "Shit. I forgot to tell you. Anna asked if I'd go to the movie with her. Since you were grounded, I said yes."

I try to make my expression neutral, like it's no big deal. They're friends. That's a thing that friends do together, right? They go to the movies. They hang out. There's absolutely no reason for me to be angry.

"Oh, really? Well, actually, my dad ungrounded me. So I can go." I fix my eyes on Anna to see if this news disappoints her. She doesn't bat an eyelash.

"Great," she says. "So I guess I'll see you tomorrow."

"I guess so."

"Well, then. Later." She flips her hair and winks at Rollins before turning to leave. Really? Who *winks* at their friends?

I don't have time to get bent out of shape about the wink, though, because Rollins enfolds me in his arms. He stuffs his hands into my back pockets and snuggles close for a kiss. I'd be lying if I said I didn't wish Anna would turn around right now and see us.

"Mmmmm, I'm glad your dad ungrounded you," he whispers in my ear.

"Me too."

I'm enjoying the feeling of Rollins's breath against my neck when I notice Regina farther down the hall, shoving her backpack into her locker. I break away from Rollins. "Hey, I'm going to be late. See you at lunch?"

"Wouldn't miss it."

Regina looks up as I approach her. Am I imagining things, or does guilt flit across her face? She turns back to her locker, looking into the magnetic mirror stuck on the door, fluffing her hair. It's fallen flat from the rain, and no amount of fluffing will save it.

"So I hear you went to visit Scotch yesterday."

"Oh, yeah. I just wanted to see how he was doing." She won't look at me.

"And how is he?"

"Still unconscious. But I talked to him for a long time. And once, I swear, he squeezed my hand."

"So did you meet his parents?"

She shakes her head quickly. "No, they'd gone home for a while. His mom was really tired. My mom was the same way when my brother died. It's just exhausting, to maintain that level of worry for an extended period of time."

"I'm surprised the nurses let you in to see him. Isn't he in intensive care?"

"Well, I might have told them I was his little sister."

"You know his parents will be looking for you now. Not only did a mysterious girl call to report Scotch's whereabouts, but now the nurses will be able to describe what you look like to his mom and dad when they find out you were there. And they *will* find out."

Regina freezes. Obviously, this hadn't occurred to her.

"Be careful," I say. "Samantha's on the warpath. She's pissed about you going to visit Scotch."

Regina shrugs. "I'm tired of Samantha thinking she can rule the world." With that, she slams her locker and walks away.

In English, Mrs. Winger asks us to get together with our partners to work on our essays. I take the desk next to Samantha's. She's dressed in an uncharacteristically muted fashion today, with a plain blue T-shirt, jeans, and no makeup. Her hair is pulled back in a ponytail, and I can tell from the circles under her eyes that she didn't sleep much last night. We have that in common.

"I just saw Regina in the hall," I say when Mrs. Winger ducks out of the room to go make copies of a worksheet. "I told her she needs to be more careful."

"Lot of good that does now," Samantha says under her breath. "Did you see the cops in the cafeteria this morning? They're still questioning people. It's only a matter of time before they get to Regina. She'll cave under the pressure."

"I don't think she's going to say anything," I say to appease Samantha, even though I'm not entirely sure about that.

Samantha closes her eyes. "Ugh, I just want to forget the whole thing ever happened. I want to think about normal things like which cheer we're going to do at halftime or what's going to happen next on *The Vampire Diaries*."

"Same here," I say. "You know, a bunch of us are going to the new *Scar* movie tomorrow night. Do you want to come?" Since Anna is coming, I figure it's not really a double date anymore. Might as well invite one more person. The more, the merrier, and all. Besides, I think it'll do Samantha some good.

"A bunch of us, meaning who?"

"Mattie, Russ White, Rollins. And this girl Rollins works with at the radio station, Anna." I wrinkle my nose when I say Anna's name.

"I take it we're not a fan of Anna?"

I sigh. "It's just . . . Rollins and I have kind of taken things to the next level. And Anna seems to keep getting in the way. They're just friends, but . . . I wish she weren't so pretty."

"Say no more," Samantha says. "You've come to the right person. I'm going to pick you up after cheerleading practice, and we're going to the mall. Before the movie I'll give you one of my famous makeovers, and when I'm through with you, Rollins won't know what hit him." I feel a bit ill, thinking about Samantha's last "famous makeover," but her cheeks have gotten a bit rosier in the last few minutes. If finding me some new lipstick will take her mind off everything that's been happening, then why not?

"Ugh. Okay."

She slaps me on the back.

"Get ready to meet your inner vixen."

———

I'm waiting for Rollins by his locker after school when Mattie taps me on the shoulder. "Hey," she says, readjusting the strap of the duffel bag in which she keeps all of her cheerleading stuff.

"Hey," I say, picking some nonexistent fuzz off the sleeve of my hoodie.

"I hear Samantha is taking you to the mall after practice. You mind if I come with?"

I sigh. "Honestly, Mattie, I'm still kind of pissed that you and Lydia seem to be sharing everything with each other lately. Why would you keep that stuff about Lydia and Dad dating in high school a secret from me?"

Mattie touches my sleeve. "I'm sorry. I should have told you. But I knew you'd make a big thing out of it, and I . . . I just like having her around. Can't you forgive me?"

I look into Mattie's eyes. I'm tired of this tension between us.

"Okay."

Mattie's whole face lights up, and she draws me into a bear hug.

"I'll see you after practice. We'll find something really cute for you to wear."

I groan. "I can't wait."

CHAPTER TWENTY-SIX

The parking lot at the mall is crammed with cars. Samantha parks at the far end. I climb out of the car at the same time Mattie pops out of the back. I feel as though I'm doing a death march as I walk toward JCPenney.

I'd rather be doing anything else than letting Samantha dress me up as her own personal Barbie doll. Well, I suppose hanging out at home with Lydia would be worse. So at least there's that.

Samantha leads us to Forever 21 and makes a beeline for a display of baby tees. She selects a silver top, while Mattie fingers a purple one. They are talking, laughing. It's good to see them carefree for a change.

"What do you think of this?" Mattie asks, holding up the shirt.

"I don't think . . ."

The clothes in this store are most definitely *not me*. But Sam and Mattie don't pay any attention. They prance around, picking out a pink tank top and a lacy white button-down to put over it with a very short jean skirt.

Mattie pushes me toward the dressing room.

"Seriously?" I ask.

Samantha gives me a stern look. "Trust me."

I roll my eyes and carry the garments into the dressing room. Shimmying out of my torn jeans, I glance in the mirror. My legs appear to be thinner—they're almost bony, with knobby knees poking out. When I pull off my T-shirt, I am struck by my lack of a chest.

An annoying thought buzzes around the back of my brain: *You know who has a great body? ANNA.* I tell my brain to shove it, but it does no good. A feeling of self-consciousness has settled over me as I think about going to the movie with Rollins and Anna tomorrow night. *He only likes her as a friend,* I remind myself, pulling on the skirt and top.

When I emerge, tugging at the uncomfortably snug clothing, Mattie claps her hands. "Yes," she cries. "Just, yes. You have to get this."

Samantha nods her approval. "My work here is done."

I turn and study myself in the full-length mirror. The girl looking back at me seems familiar, like a girl I once knew but forgot long ago. Her long, blond hair falls around her face in wisps. Her cheeks are the same pink of the tank top. Her legs look kind of silly in a miniskirt and Converse shoes, but lovely just the same.

Mattie puts her hand on my shoulder. "It's perfect."

"You think so?"

Samantha opens her purse and whips out a credit card. "Vee, let me buy it for you."

"Don't you mean let *your parents* buy it?"

She shrugs. "I get a clothing allowance. This won't even make a dent in it. Besides, I didn't get you anything for your birthday this year."

I don't want to make waves.

"Whatever," I say. "That's fine. Let's just get it and go." Mattie and Samantha beam, irritating me. "I'll go change."

When I return, Samantha is at the register with Mattie and an armload of clothes she seems to have gathered in the thirty seconds I was in the dressing room.

"Could you add these things, too, please?" Samantha sweetly asks the clerk. She takes the clothes out of my hands and puts them on the counter.

The saleslady folds the outfit neatly, slips it into a plastic bag, and hands it over to Samantha, who in turn passes it to me. I hold it at arm's length.

"Shouldn't we be getting home soon? Dad will be wondering where we are," I say. I can't wait to get out of this place.

Mattie checks the time on her phone. "Oh, you're right. Let's go."

As we pass by the food court, I get the strangest feeling that someone is watching us. My eyes pass over the line of teenagers at Cinnabon, the haggard mother dragging three children behind her, the man eating Chinese and reading a paperback novel, finally coming to rest on the fountain in the center of everything.

There's someone on the other side of the fountain.

A woman with graying hair pulled into a bun.

She is now standing and grabbing her purse and ducking her head down, probably hoping that I don't recognize her. But I do.

It's Diane.

Again.

What is she doing here?

She turns away before I can call her name.

Sitting in the back of the car, I tune Mattie and Samantha out as they excitedly discuss tomorrow's plans. The outfit that Samantha bought for me is draped over my lap. I dig my fingers into the plastic, trying to make sense out of what just happened.

Why would Diane be following me?

I must have a strained look on my face because my sister glances back at me and frowns. "What's wrong?"

I try to smile. "Oh, nothing. I just realized I have a Psych test on Monday. Totally haven't studied for it."

Samantha looks at me in the rearview mirror but doesn't say anything.

"Well," Mattie says breezily, "you have all weekend. Don't worry about it."

"Yeah," I say.

It was just a coincidence, I tell myself. *Nothing more.*

Deep down, though, I know I've seen Diane too many times in the past week for it to be a coincidence.

Saturday night. I stare with dismay into the full-length mirror on the back of my door. Against my better judgment,

I let Samantha do my hair and makeup. She's curled and teased my hair within an inch of its life. It literally does not move when I touch it. Eye shadow is layered from eyeball to eyebrow. She even pressed on fake eyelashes, which are itchy. Every time I fiddle with them, though, Samantha yells at me.

"What do you think?" Samantha asks, standing back to admire her work.

"It's . . . great," I say.

"You look gorgeous, Vee," Mattie says. She's wearing some skinny jeans and a low-cut tank top.

"I feel like a different person."

And I'm not sure that's a good thing.

The doorbell rings.

"That must be them," Mattie says excitedly. She grabs her purse from the top of my desk and checks herself in the mirror one last time before opening the door. Samantha and I follow her downstairs, where my dad is standing with Russ and Rollins.

For a split second, I am nearly paralyzed with guilt. Here I am, about to go to a movie with my friends, while Scotch is lying unconscious in the hospital—because of me. I shake my head to make the thought go away. There's nothing I can do for him now.

Not tonight.

Rollins's eyes sweep over my body as I come down the stairs, then back up, resting on my face. I can't tell what he's thinking. His face is unreadable.

"Remember your curfew," my father warns. "Midnight.

Not one second later."

Mattie gives my dad a kiss on the cheek, and we all head outside. Russ's and Rollins's vehicles are both in the driveway. Mattie opens the passenger door of Russ's silver pickup. Samantha walks to her own car, which is parked in the street.

"We've got to pick up Anna on the way," Rollins says. He climbs into his car and turns the key. I get in and pull the seat belt over my lap, trying not to notice the way my boobs are practically popping out of my shirt.

"You look different," Rollins says.

"Is that a good thing or a bad thing?" I ask.

"I guess I mean . . . You look the same as everyone else. I can hardly recognize you under all that makeup."

A bad thing, I think.

"Samantha gave me a makeover," I say.

"Ah," Rollins replies, looking over his shoulder as he pulls out of the driveway. He doesn't say anything else on the way to Anna's house.

CHAPTER TWENTY-SEVEN

The six of us stand in the lobby of the movie theater—Russ, Mattie, Rollins, Anna, Samantha, and me. It's a strange grouping, and there are a few moments of awkward silence as we try to think of something to talk about. My mind keeps returning to Scotch, but I can't bring him up in front of Russ and Anna.

"Well, shall we?" Russ asks Mattie finally, gesturing toward the ticket window. Russ digs out his wallet and retrieves a twenty-dollar bill.

The rest of us pay for our own tickets and head to the snack counter. Anna announces that she'll buy the popcorn. Samantha gets some strawberry Twizzlers. I buy a small Mountain Dew, allowing myself a little caffeine to stay awake during the movie. We carry our loot into the theater.

Russ and Mattie take seats up front, where they can kick their legs up on the railing. They look like a real couple already, laughing and sharing popcorn. I feel a pang of jealousy when I have to follow Rollins and Anna to the back row, where Rollins and I usually sit so we can make fun of movies without people yelling at us. Samantha trails behind me.

Anna edges her way down the row first, and Rollins goes next. I take a seat on his other side and slouch down. My skirt rides up embarrassingly high, and I yank it so it covers my thighs. Samantha flops into the chair on my other side, already chewing on a Twizzler.

The lights dim, and the previews come up. Rollins has the popcorn in his lap, and I'm conscious of every time Anna reaches over to grab a handful. I watch out of the corner of my eye to make sure her hand doesn't linger and brush against his. They both seem oblivious to my angst, though. Slowly, my attention moves away from Anna's and Rollins's hands dipping repeatedly into the popcorn.

Onscreen, a beautiful girl with dark brown hair is in the shower, lathering shampoo into her hair. Her eyes are closed, and she doesn't see the shadow that moves across the bright orange shower curtain. She starts to sing a pop song, belting the lyrics over the sound of the cascading water.

Mattie, several rows ahead of me, hides her face against Russ's shoulder. He raises his arm and wraps it around her.

After her shower, the girl in the movie throws open the curtain and steps into the bathroom. She reaches for a towel and wraps it around her. Through the steamy bathroom mirror, we see her take a step toward the closed door. She reaches out her hand, gets ready to open it.

Someone in the front shouts, "Don't do it!"

But of course she does.

She opens the door, and there the killer is, wearing a clown mask.

The girl screams, takes a step backward, stumbles on the bath mat, and falls. We see the shiny steel raise into the air. And lower. Again and again.

Without thinking, I reach over and grab Rollins's sleeve. My eyes are glued to the screen.

The last shot is of the knife, speckled with dots of red. Then the title sequence begins. My heart is thumping under my shirt, even though I've seen the previous *Scar* movies and anticipated what was going to happen. There's something about seeing a movie in the theater, as opposed to my own living room. Makes it scarier. More delicious.

I'm just about to lean over and tell Rollins as much when I realize I'm not the only one grabbing on to him. On his other side, Anna is clutching Rollins's bicep and averting her eyes from the screen. And Rollins has a half smile on his face, as if he's enjoying it.

I choose this moment to go to the ladies' room. I'm so upset, I almost trip over Samantha while I'm rushing to get out of the theater. I hurry out the door, and the brightness of the hallway makes me squint. I'm disoriented for a moment, but then I see the sign for the women's room.

Inside, I take my time. My face is wet, and I realize I've been crying, which just makes me even angrier because some girl grabbing Rollins's arm is nothing to cry about. I unroll a few squares of toilet paper and use it to wipe my face off, then flush it down the toilet.

When I open the stall door, I come face-to-face with Mattie, her brow furrowed with worry. "I saw you running out of the theater. I wanted to make sure everything was okay. Are you all right?"

I sniff, hoping she can't tell I've been crying. I'm supposed to be the tough one. I'm supposed to take care of *her*. But look at me now, standing here in my too-tight pink tank top and too-short skirt, crying over a guy. I feel like I don't even know who I am anymore. I knew I shouldn't have worn this stupid outfit.

"Yeah, I'm fine," I say, pushing past her to the sink. "I guess I'm just not really in the mood for a scary movie."

After drying my hands, I throw the wadded-up paper towel in the trash. I turn around to look at Mattie, who's folded her arms across her chest.

"Don't give me that crap. What happened?"

I sigh in exasperation. "It's just—Rollins and I always go to these movies together, and all of a sudden Anna's in the picture. He says she's just a friend, but it seems like she's always around. I know she likes him . . ."

Mattie squeezes my shoulder. "You know Rollins isn't into Anna. He's been in love with you ever since he laid eyes on you, practically. A blind person could see that."

Her words confirm what Rollins has already said to me, but I can't accept them, for some reason. Maybe it's because Rollins said yes to Anna's invitation when it should be obvious to anyone that it would hurt me. Maybe it's the expression on his face when she clung to his arm during the murder scene.

Mattie pulls me toward the door. "Now can I get back to my date? Russ threatened to eat all of the popcorn if I was gone too long."

I resist. "You go ahead. I just need to be alone for a few minutes." *In case I start crying again,* I think, but there's no way I'm going to say that out loud.

Mattie gives me a reproachful look but lets go of me. "Okay. Don't take too long, though. Feeling sorry for yourself isn't going to make this situation any better."

She leaves me, but her words remain. Mattie is right, of course. It's not going to do me any good to sit here in the bathroom and bawl all night.

I take a deep breath.

Then I straighten my skirt and walk out of the bathroom, wobbling a little on the high heels Samantha and Mattie insisted I wear.

Anna manages to refrain from touching Rollins for the rest of the movie. Not that I'm keeping track or anything. The lights go on, and I stand up quickly, grabbing my empty cup so I can dump it in the trash on the way out.

Russ and Mattie wait for us at the front of the theater.

Samantha yawns. "That was boring."

"It was okay," Russ replies, "but it's no *Evil Dead II*."

Rollins slaps Russ on the back. "I knew there was a reason I liked you."

Mattie holds her cell phone, scrolling through messages. From the look on her face, I can tell something's wrong. I let Rollins and Anna head toward the exit without me so

I can see what's going on. Russ follows, claiming he has to use the bathroom.

I touch Mattie's elbow.

She looks up. "Regina texted me."

Samantha suddenly looks very alert.

"And?"

Mattie looks at us with wide eyes.

"Scotch is awake."

CHAPTER TWENTY-EIGHT

I am silent on the ride home.

Dread claws at my stomach. If Scotch is awake, he could be talking. If he's talking, he might be telling everyone exactly what happened that night at Lookout Point. I made Mattie call Regina back to ask for more details, but it went straight to voice mail. I have to get home as soon as possible and slide into Scotch so I can find out what's going on.

Anna and Rollins don't seem to notice my preoccupation. They are heatedly discussing the plot twist at the end of the movie. Rollins insists he saw it coming a mile away, and Anna says he's full of shit.

"Can you take me home first?" I ask, interrupting.

Rollins glances over at me. "I thought we were going to go get coffee or something?"

I grimace. "I've got a headache."

That much is true. The combination of listening to Anna and Rollins flirtatiously banter about the movie and my torturous thoughts about what Scotch might be telling the police this very second has given me a massive migraine.

It is clear from his one raised eyebrow that Rollins doesn't believe me, but he steers the car toward my house. Anna is oblivious and continues with the conversation as if I hadn't spoken at all.

Rollins pulls into my driveway a few moments later, and Anna pauses long enough for me to say good night. When I get out, she gets out of the back of the car and sits in the passenger seat. That is enough to make me regret telling Rollins to take me home first. Now it's just the two of them with hours to kill. I wonder if they'll go have coffee. Or maybe they'll go someplace more intimate.

I can't think about that now. I push the thought out of my head.

Inside, Mattie is sitting in the kitchen, filling Lydia in on her date. When she sees me lingering in the doorway, she excuses herself and pulls me into the foyer.

"It's about time," she says.

"Did Regina call you back?"

"No. I've tried over and over. She's not answering. Samantha said she'd stop by Regina's house on the way home. Vee, I'm scared. Do you think Scotch remembers what happened? What if he talks to the police? Tells them you were there?"

Even though Mattie is voicing my worst fear, I try to appear calm. I know how frightened she is by the possibility of me getting in trouble. I have a way to check and see what's going on, but I can't let Mattie in on my secret. She's already too involved in this mess.

"I'm sure everything will be okay," I assure her. "He probably doesn't even remember what happened."

Mattie gives me a doubtful look.

"Even if he does remember, what are the police going to do? Arrest me for playing a prank?" I don't want to tell Mattie that Scotch might be telling the cops something worse. He could very well be telling them I pushed him off the cliff. After all, I wasn't exactly myself. Maybe I did. Or whoever was in my body did.

Lydia steps out from the shadows.

I wonder how long she's been standing there, whether she heard anything significant. "Come on, let's go to bed." I take a few steps toward the staircase. Reluctantly, Mattie follows.

"Good night, girls," Lydia says.

"Good night," Mattie replies.

I don't respond.

It takes Mattie forever to fall asleep. She keeps flipping from one side to the other and sighing. Finally, sometime after two in the morning, I hear her snore. For a moment, I debate staying in my room to slide into Scotch. After all, Mattie is asleep. But I don't want her to wake up and disturb me in the middle of my investigation.

I reach under my pillow and pull out the piece of purple fabric from my old Homecoming dress that I stashed there earlier. The whole house is silent as I tiptoe out of my room and down the hall. I pause just outside of Mattie's room, checking to make sure there's no light shining under the door. Lydia seems to be sleeping, though. Or lying there very, very quietly.

I lock myself in the bathroom. After climbing into the tub, I pull the shower curtain closed behind me. I grip the tattered piece of cloth to my chest and close my eyes, hoping that the caffeine from the pop I had at the movie has worn off enough to let me slide. Deliberately, I slow my breathing. The tub is cool against my skin, and I feel goosebumps pop up on my arms.

Long moments pass.

I open my eyes, transfer the silky material from one hand to another.

Wait.

Rub the cloth against my cheek.

Wait some more.

Nothing happens.

I'm sure an hour has passed—maybe two—when I finally give up. Defeated, I pull back the curtain and hoist myself out of the tub. The piece from the dress is wadded in my fist, sweaty and wrinkled. It seems to be useless. Or maybe it's me. I could just be too worked up to slide.

I unlock the door, flip off the light on my way out.

When I am halfway to my bedroom, I hear something downstairs. It sounds like a key jiggling in a lock. The next sound is unmistakable—the front door opening. I hustle into my bedroom and pull the door closed behind me. Press my ear to the door.

Footsteps coming up the steps. They're soft but most definitely there.

Is it my father? Was he called to the hospital in the middle of the night for an emergency? Usually he stomps up the stairs, the noise surprisingly loud for a thin man.

The footsteps reach the hallway. I hold my breath, waiting to hear them move away from me and then my father's door clicking shut.

But that's not what happens.

The footsteps move toward me, slowly but surely.

They move closer and closer until I'm sure the person is standing right outside my door and I imagine I can hear them breathing, inches away, with only a thin piece of wood between us.

Then the person continues on down the hall, past the bathroom. I hear Mattie's door open and close. And then silence.

It was Lydia.

I glance at the clock on my nightstand. It's after three.

What was she doing outside in the middle of the night?

The next morning, I find my father, Mattie, and Lydia in the kitchen. I grab a banana and lean against the counter. Lydia is sitting at the kitchen table, wearing my dad's bathrobe. There are dark circles under her eyes. She sips wearily at her cup of coffee.

My father doesn't look any better. He moves around the kitchen slowly, grabbing a cereal bowl, a box of Cheerios, and milk from the refrigerator. Mattie watches him, and then says, "Dad, you look like you had a rough night."

"One of my patients had a heart attack," he says. He turns his attention to Lydia. "Thanks for giving me a ride, by the way. One of the nurses dropped me off when her shift was done. I'm going to have to buy a car this weekend. I can't keep relying on other people to drive me around."

"It's no problem," Lydia says. "My pleasure."

Hmmmmm. So that's what she was doing last night? Driving my father to the hospital?

"I guess we're not going to make it to nine o'clock mass," my dad says, pouring himself a bowl of cereal.

Lydia taps her coffee cup thoughtfully. "Don't they also have an eleven o'clock mass?"

"Yes, they do. Would you like to go?"

Lydia smiles. "Sure."

"Mattie, how about you?"

My father doesn't ask me. I haven't been to church in years.

"Sure," Mattie says. She's finished her bowl of cereal and is now drinking the milk out of the bottom of the bowl. "I'll go get dressed."

Taking the last bite of my banana, I throw the peel away.

I wait for Mattie to rinse her bowl and put it in the dishwasher, and then I pull her into the hall. "Did Regina ever call back?" I ask in a low tone.

Looking troubled, Mattie shakes her head. "I called Samantha to see if she talked to her, but her phone went to voice mail, too."

"Shit."

I figure I'll try to slide into Scotch once more after everyone leaves for church, but what if I can't?

Mattie must notice my troubled expression because she reaches out and grabs my arm. "Hey, remember what you said last night? Don't worry. You're not going to get arrested just for playing a prank. Right?"

I paste a smile on my face.

"Right."

After my dad, Lydia, and Mattie leave for church, I grab the piece of purple cloth and lie down on my bed, willing myself to slide into Scotch. But it's just like last night. No matter what position I get into or how I slow my breathing, nothing happens.

I groan and toss the fabric on the floor.

The doorbell rings.

I sit up.

Who could be at our door on a Sunday morning?

As I hurry down the stairs, I wonder if it's Regina. Maybe she came over to tell Mattie and me about what happened with Scotch at the hospital. I throw open the door, hoping to see her on the other side.

But it's not Regina.

It's Rollins, and it's clear from the look on his face that something's wrong.

"Can I come inside?" He runs his fingers through his hair nervously. I realize that, since he dropped me off, I haven't even thought about him driving around with Anna last night. As I study his anxious face, I am overcome with apprehension. *Did* something happen? Did they kiss? Something more?

"Sure," I say, holding the door open for him.

He wanders past me and turns to go into the living room. I close the door and follow him. When he sinks into my father's recliner and covers his face with his hands, I feel my heart start to pound. Whatever he has to tell me must be terrible for him to act this way.

"Just say it," I murmur, keeping my voice neutral as I sit down on the couch. I prepare myself for the worst. *He's in love with her. I knew it.*

He pulls his hands away from his face. "Vee, we're in real trouble."

Just get it over with.

"What's going on?" I ask, unable to keep the panic from seeping into my voice. "What is it?"

He swallows. "Scotch is dead."

The room starts to close in on me.

"I—I don't understand."

"My uncle came home from his shift a half hour ago. He said something crazy was going on at the hospital and asked if I knew a kid from school named Scott Becker."

Suddenly I can't breathe.

"How did he die?"

Rollins is quiet for a moment before answering.

"He was smothered. With a pillow."

"When?"

"They're not sure, exactly. He was alive when the night nurse last checked on him, a little after midnight. When the morning nurse went in at six, he was gone."

My mind is racing. I think about last night, how I tried to use the piece of my dress to slide into Scotch. Nothing had happened. It wasn't because I lost my ability. It's because there was no one to slide into.

Scotch was dead already.

CHAPTER TWENTY-NINE

Rollins and I sit on the steps of my front porch, waiting for my family to return. He holds my right hand in between both of his. Though it is a warm day for April, in the midseventies, I can't stop shivering.

I texted Mattie a couple of times, not wanting to interrupt mass, but when she didn't answer I went ahead and called her. She didn't pick up. Rollins convinced me that she just had her phone on vibrate and didn't notice it ringing.

With nothing else to do with my nervous energy, I bounce my legs up and down. "What am I going to tell Mattie?" I wonder aloud.

Rollins traces my palm with one finger. "I think you're going to have to tell her the truth," he says quietly. "All of it."

I know what he means. I have to tell everything, starting with the sliding. I've been meaning to tell Mattie about my secret for a long time. I just didn't want her to give me the same reaction my father gave me when I tried to tell him all those years ago. Mattie has always looked up to me. I didn't want her to think I'm nuts. But if I'm going to solve Scotch's murder, I'm going to need all the help I can get.

"You're right," I say.

Lydia's car turns the corner, and I jump to my feet. The front two doors swing open, and my father emerges from the driver's seat. Lydia gets out on the passenger's side. It takes everything within me to conceal the uneasiness I feel at the sight of her. I can't shake the feeling that she might have had something to do with Scotch's death, especially since she was at the hospital last night.

I wait for Mattie to get out, but the two back doors remain shut. Taking a few steps toward the car, I realize there's no one in the backseat.

"Where's Mattie?" I demand.

My father holds the front door open for Lydia. "She went over to Regina's house. It's so gorgeous out, she wanted to walk. She said Regina's parents would drive her home later."

I groan.

"What? What's the matter?"

Inside the house, Lydia is watching me.

"Nothing. I was just—she forgot that she was supposed to help me with a school project this afternoon."

"Oh."

"Rollins . . ." I turn to face him.

Rollins must read the struggle behind my eyes. I need

to go find Mattie, but I don't want to leave my father here with Lydia. He leans over and gives me a kiss on the cheek. "I'll go find her," he whispers in my ear. He starts to walk in the direction of his car, but I grab him and pull him into a kiss. He is rigid at first, probably shocked that I'd lay one on him right in front of my father and aunt, but then he cups my chin and kisses me back.

When we part, he says softly, "I'll be right back."

Turning back toward the door, I see the strained look on my father's face. "Really? Did I need to see that?"

"Sorry, Dad," I say, trying to sound natural. I'm not quite sure I pull it off.

I step inside the door, and my father pushes it closed.

Lydia smiles at me. "So what were you up to while we were gone? You know, my parents would have killed me if I had a boy over while they were out."

I scowl at her.

My father turns to me. "You know, your aunt has a point. It didn't bother me so much when you and Rollins were just friends, but it's clear that you guys have gotten, um, *closer* in the past week and I'm just not that comfortable with—"

I raise my hand to stop him. I don't feel like getting into a fight over this right now. "It's fine, Dad. I won't have Rollins over when you're gone. Okay?"

My father looks surprised, like he wasn't expecting me to give in so easily. "All right, then. Good. Do you want me to make you some lunch?"

"I'm not hungry."

"Okay. Well, ladies, I'm beat. I think I'm going to catch a few winks." My father heads up the stairs.

I clear my throat. "Actually, Dad, I need to talk to you. *Both* of you." I throw a glance at Lydia, who eyes me nervously. It occurs to me that she probably hasn't filled my father in yet and thinks I'm going to spill her little secret, that she has a fiancé back in California.

My father rubs his eyes wearily. "Okay."

Lydia and my father follow me into the living room and sit down on the couch. I remain standing and cross my arms over my chest before saying, "You know, Rollins's uncle works at the hospital. That's why he was over here this morning."

My father exhales loudly. "I'm sorry, Vee. I was going to tell you. I was just trying to think of the right way to do it."

Lydia looks from my father to me, confused. "What happened?" I try to figure out whether she's acting or if she really doesn't know about Scotch's death.

"Scott Becker is dead," my father tells Lydia. "It seems he was murdered last night." He turns to me. "I'm sorry you had to hear that from Rollins."

Lydia's mouth turns into an O of shock. "He was murdered? How terrible!"

I turn to her. "*You* were at the hospital last night, weren't you?"

"Sylvia," my father says, a warning in his voice.

Lydia's eyebrow twitches. "Are you insinuating something?"

"Why? Did you do something wrong?"

Lydia flinches as if I slapped her. "Vee, how could you ever think I would kill someone?" she asks.

"I don't know. Why would you show up on our doorstep after twenty years? Why would you leave behind a fiancé without telling him where you were? Why would you use a fake name in California? Face it: I know almost nothing about you. How am I supposed to believe anything you say?" My words get louder and louder until they turn into a shout.

Lydia's nostrils flare. "Sylvia Bell, I admit I'm no saint. I've done a lot of things in my life that I'm not proud of, but I can't believe you could ever think I'd kill a teenage boy."

Without another word, she turns and runs up the steps. Moments later, I hear Mattie's door slam shut.

My father's mouth is hanging open, like he's not sure what just happened. "Lydia . . . has a fiancé?"

"Yeah," I say softly. "In California. They were supposed to be married last week. Are you . . . are you okay?"

He shakes his head. "Of course. I'm just surprised. Why wouldn't I be okay?"

"Because you still love her?"

"Oh, Vee. I don't love Lydia. We only dated for a couple of weeks. Until I met your mom. Come here." He motions for me to sit next to him on the couch. When I sink into the seat beside him, he wraps his arm around me. "I'm sorry I didn't tell you."

"Why didn't you?"

"I thought it would be weird."

"It is weird," I say. "So you really don't have feelings for her anymore? You've been spending a lot of time together."

"Well, she *is* family. I want her to have a good life and everything. That's why I've been letting her stay here. But I have no interest in her romantically."

I breathe a sigh of relief. "That's good to know." My thoughts turn back to Scotch's death. I realize that my father was at the hospital last night when Scotch died. Maybe he knows whether that weird lady, Diane, was working last night.

"Dad . . ." I venture. "Do you know a nurse named Diane? She wears a bun all the time?"

"That's a huge change in topic. Why do you ask?"

I search my brain for a reason I'd know that she worked at the hospital. "Well, remember the lady who gave me a ride home after my car accident? I ran into her at the mall last night, and I was chatting with her. It turns out that she works at the hospital. So . . . do you know her?"

"Sure I do," my father says, arranging a pillow behind him. "Diane Acton? She works in the intensive care unit. Has for a long time, ever since I've worked there. In fact, she was friends with your mother."

"What?" I say, pulling away from him. I'm not sure what to make of this new information.

"Yeah, your mom didn't have many friends, but she sure

liked Diane. I'm not sure what they had in common. Every time I've ever talked to Diane, she's seemed pretty eccentric to me. But I thought it was nice that your mother had someone to confide in."

At that moment, the front door opens.

CHAPTER THIRTY

I jump off the couch and run into the front entryway. Mattie walks in, looking pale. Rollins follows close behind, holding her elbow to steady her. From the looks on both their faces, I'm pretty sure Rollins already broke the news about Scotch's death.

"We'll be up in my room," I call to my father.

The three of us climb the stairs and shuffle wordlessly into my bedroom. I lock the door behind us and then turn to face Mattie, who sinks onto my bed. Rollins sits in the rocking chair, looking nervous.

"What did Regina have to say?" I ask.

Mattie shakes her head. "No one was home."

"Matt, I have to tell you something."

"Rollins already told me about Scotch," Mattie replies. Her eyes are slightly glazed.

"It's something else," I say gently. "Something about me. I've been keeping a secret from you," I say.

Mattie's forehead wrinkles. "What is it?"

Clearing my throat, I try to think of the best way to

explain. Mattie was so young when all of this started. I don't know if she even remembers those days when I first started passing out. Or the fight I had with my father when he wouldn't believe what was really happening to me and he decided to send me to a shrink.

"Okay. I know you were young, but do you remember when I told Dad that something strange was happening to me when I passed out?"

Mattie shakes her head.

"I don't have narcolepsy. When I pass out, I go somewhere else. It just depends on what I'm touching at the time. Say I'm touching Dad's watch. That means I'll slide into Dad and see through his eyes, whatever he's doing. Only it can't just be any item. It has to be something that's important to the person. Something they've emotionally imprinted on."

"I don't understand," she says. "This doesn't make any sense."

"I know. It doesn't make any sense, but it's true. And the weirdest part is that I've learned how to control it. I can take over a person's brain and make them do things, say things. I can *control* them."

"What are you talking about?"

Taking a deep breath, I tell myself it's okay. I knew this was going to be hard. Mattie will have to see it to believe it.

I pull open the bottom drawer of my dresser and search through the things I've accumulated over the past few months, the things that allow me to slide. I grab the Smashing Pumpkins T-shirt Rollins gave to me last fall.

He left an emotional imprint on it that allowed me to slide into him a few times. When I explained about my ability and that I saw his miserable home life through his eyes, he accused me of invading his privacy. Since then, I've never slid into Rollins again.

Not until now.

I hold the shirt up to Rollins, a question in my eyes. His face tightens, but then he nods. It's the only way for me to convince Mattie. I have to demonstrate my power. With the T-shirt crumpled in my hands, I sit next to Mattie on the bed.

"I know it's confusing. Just watch, though."

I arrange myself so I'm lying on my bed, cradling the T-shirt against my chest. I think back to the day Rollins gave me the shirt, how happy I was. I'd wanted it for such a long time. I was confused the first time I slid into Rollins because I didn't understand why he would be emotionally attached to a gift for me. He'd kept his feelings for me a secret. But now I know, and it feels strange to slide into him, almost intimate.

My perspective shifts. I am in the same room, but seeing through Rollins's eyes. He is still sitting in the rocking chair, facing my bed. Mattie is gaping at my unconscious form, which is sprawled out with the Smashing Pumpkins T-shirt.

"Mattie," I whisper. "It's me."

Mattie looks at Rollins, confused, like she's not sure what he's talking about. I need to give her some evidence to prove that it's really me.

"It's me. Sylvia." I rack my brain, trying to think of some obscure piece of trivia about Mattie that only I, her sister, would know. "All right, how about this? I know that you threw up in Matthew Baker's hair in the second grade. You were so embarrassed because you had the biggest crush on him."

Mattie's face scrunches. "Why are you guys playing tricks on me at a time like this? It isn't funny!"

"Shhhhhhhh," I say, getting out of the chair and going over to her. "It's not a trick. It's really me."

She glares. "You guys are sick."

"Look. How about this? You ask me a question, something no one else could know. Something only I would know."

"Something Vee would know?"

"Exactly."

Mattie looks down. I see her face change. When she raises her head, I see a challenge in her eyes. "Before Mom died, what did she give me to remember her by?"

Yes. This is something I know. "She gave you that necklace," I say, pointing. "You never take it off because you're afraid that if you do, you'll forget her completely."

I can see the tears in Mattie's eyes, threatening to spill. She comes close to me and studies my face intently. "Vee?"

My face breaks into a grin. "You got it!"

She throws her arms around me—well, Rollins, really. I can feel her breath, hot in my ear. "It's true then. It's really true."

"Of course it's true. Did you think I was lying?"

And then she really is crying, her whole body shaking against me. "It's just that—I thought . . . I thought I was going crazy."

"You're not crazy."

"I didn't know what was happening to me . . ." Mattie says, her voice breaking. "I was having such weird dreams. And then things were happening. My dreams were coming true."

Now it's my turn to be baffled.

"What are you talking about?" I say, pushing her back so I can see her face. She is crying freely now, and I can hardly make out her words.

"First there was that car accident. And I thought it was just a coincidence. But then I dreamed of Lookout Point, and I thought there was something really wrong with me."

I grab hold of her face and make her look at me. "Slow down. Tell me everything."

She gasps for air. I wait for her to catch her breath. Then she speaks. "Vee, I was there the night that Scotch fell."

I take a step back, covering my mouth. "What?"

She starts to cry. "What do you call it, sliding? I can do it, too."

My knees buckle, and I sink to the floor. She collapses next to me, and we sit there, clutching each other.

She explains how it started a few months ago. She was having strange dreams that she was other people, doing ordinary, mundane things. She dreamed of my father brushing his teeth. She dreamed of me, taking notes in English class. The dreams were strangely vivid, but she didn't think anything of them until the night I got into a car accident.

That night, she dreamed she woke up in my room. The radio was on, so she turned it off. She went down to the kitchen and stared at the moon through the window for a long time. Then she had a crazy idea. The dream was so real, and she was able to control it. She decided to test it out. That's when she went into the garage and started my father's car. She took it for a long ride, and then the dream ended abruptly.

I shiver as she tells the story. So well I remember that night, waking up in a car that was racing down the road. I thought it was my nightmare about Zane, so I yanked the wheel. And realized it wasn't a dream. Someone slid into me and made me steal my dad's car.

It was my sister.

Mattie goes on. Next she describes sliding into my father. It was late, and he was in the living room, gazing at old pictures of our family from when our mother was still alive. Mattie felt a rage plow through her, a rage that my father refused to get past our mother's death. He kept letting his grief get in the way of really being there for us. So she grabbed our parents' wedding portrait and threw it on the floor. She kept grabbing pictures and smashing them everywhere. Then I appeared in the doorway, and all the anger fell away, and she slid back into her own body.

"And then there was Lookout Point."

Mattie takes a deep breath and explains what happened the night of Scotch's accident. She fell asleep while waiting for me, and then she found herself standing in the middle of the woods. She was confused, but she saw two beams of light shining through the trees. When she stumbled into the clearing, she saw such a beautiful vision. It was all sky, and the night was so clear that she could make out all the stars. She was filled with a deep happiness, a feeling that she was connected to everyone and everything.

"But then someone grabbed me. I turned around, and I saw that it was Scotch. I was so scared. I felt myself start to slip away. I was falling to the ground. But before I left, I heard Scotch yell, 'Get off me!'"

I stare at Mattie.

"Someone else was there, Vee. Someone *did* push Scotch."

What the hell?

"Who?" I ask.

Mattie shakes her head. "I don't know."

Frustrated, I stand up and start pacing around. I'm not used to Rollins's body, though, and I stub my toe on the rocking chair. I decide it's time to slide back into my own body.

Mattie sits on the bed and watches as I leave Rollins sitting in the rocking chair. When I am myself again, I open my eyes and see him stretching his arms over his head.

"That was weird," he says. "It was like I was floating above you guys. But everything was black. I could kind of hear you, but not really."

"Well, you missed a lot," I say. As I explain that Mattie was the one who slid into me and caused me to crash my father's car, Rollins's eyes grow large.

"You're effing kidding me."

"And she was in my body the night that Scotch fell. I mean, the night he was pushed—"

Mattie interrupts me. "Someone else was there. I mean, physically there. Someone pushed him off that cliff. I just didn't see who it was."

I flip through the possible suspects in my mind. Could it have been Lydia? Maybe it was Diane . . . ? If it was either of them, they must have driven to Lookout Point. Maybe Samantha or Regina saw a car and forgot to mention it.

"Hey, Mattie, why don't you try calling Regina again?" I suggest.

CHAPTER THIRTY-ONE

Mattie taps the pink fingernails of one hand against her skirt as she holds the phone to her ear with the other. I hear a faint ringtone. Then there's a clicking noise, and Mattie's face lights up.

"Regina? Hello, Regina?"

Mattie squints and then puts the phone down. "It's like she answered and then hung up."

"Try again," I say, irritated. We don't have time for games.

Mattie dials Regina's number again, and we all wait.

This time I hear a shriek on the other end of the line, and Mattie pulls the device away from her ear. Regina is yelling something, but I can't make out the words. Cautiously, Mattie brings the phone closer. "Slow down, Regina. I don't know what you're saying. What's wrong?"

Mattie listens for a moment.

Regina screams something else, and then there's silence.

"Could you make out anything she said?" I ask.

Mattie shakes her head. "Something about Samantha,

that we need to go to Samantha's house. What do you think is going on?"

I yank my purple hoodie out of my closet and pull it on. "I don't know. Rollins, can you drive?"

"Of course."

I take a deep breath and zip up my jacket. "Let's go."

After I unlock my door, we move into the hallway. Mattie's door is still closed. For a moment, I pause, listening to see if I can hear any movement in Mattie's room, but there is nothing. I wonder if Lydia has gone to sleep, and start to feel relieved, but then I realize a closed door isn't going to stop Lydia. If she can slide, all she needs is an item with an emotional imprint to get out of that room.

"Come on, we've got to hurry," I say under my breath. I move quickly down the stairs, with Mattie and Rollins right behind me.

My father is in his study with the door open. He's reading some medical article online.

"Hey, Dad?" Mattie says, entering the room. "We're going to Samantha's house, okay?"

"Be home by dinnertime," he replies.

"Will do."

I pull open the front door. The three of us run across the lawn and jump into Rollins's car. As soon as Mattie and I are buckled in, he backs out of the driveway. Mattie directs him toward Samantha's new house.

"What do you think is going on?" he asks.

I've been wondering the same thing. Samantha was unusually quiet last night after we got Regina's text that

Scotch had woken up. I know she's furious at Regina for hanging around the hospital. I hope we get to her house before she does anything stupid.

We pull into the parking lot, and Rollins finds a spot not far from Samantha's front door. As soon as Rollins kills the ignition, I rush out of the car. I try the doorknob, but it's locked. I start pounding on the door. "Regina? Sam, are you in there?"

No one answers.

We hear glass breaking somewhere inside.

A girl screams.

"Get back, Vee," Rollins says gruffly.

I take a step backward and stumble over a shrub. Mattie grabs my arm to steady me.

Rollins rams the door with his shoulder. It doesn't give. He tries again, this time moving back enough to give himself a running start. There's a huge crack, and the door flies open. He takes a step inside, and I follow.

There's a flight of stairs leading up.

Someone is crying. I think it's Sam, but that's crazy. Sam never cries.

Rollins takes the steps two at a time. Mattie and I are close behind. When we reach the living room, we see Regina and Samantha. They're both sobbing. Startled, Samantha turns toward us. That's when I see the gun in her hands.

I freeze, stunned.

Samantha has a wild look in her eyes. She's still in her pajamas, but she looks like she hasn't slept in days. Her hands tremble, and I pray that she won't accidentally pull the trigger.

"What the hell, Samantha?" I cry. "What's going on?"

Rollins tries to stand in front of me and Mattie. I feel Mattie grab my arm and squeeze tightly. I reciprocate.

Regina collapses onto the floor. "Samantha killed Scotch," Regina wails. "And now she's going to kill me."

"Shut up! Shut up!" Sam yells, swiveling and pointing the gun at Regina.

I take a step forward, hoping I can distract Samantha from whatever craziness she has going on in her head. "What's Regina talking about?" I ask. "Is she telling the truth?"

Samantha looks in my direction. Her eyes are not the eyes of a cold-blooded killer. She wears the expression of a frightened child.

I know Samantha.

For the longest time, she was my best friend. Practically my only friend.

She's not capable of murder.

Is she?

"What happened, Samantha?"

Not knowing where to point the gun, Samantha settles for a point between me and Regina. Rollins tries to pull me behind him, but I push his hand away.

Samantha shakes her head, tears and snot running down her face. "I had to do it," she whispers.

"Do what?"

"He wasn't supposed to wake up."

I try to process her words. It's hard to believe that Samantha was so afraid that Scotch would reveal our prank that she would kill him. "What did you think he would say, Samantha?"

"Oh, I knew he'd tell the police. He already told Regina."

Regina moans. She tries to crawl behind the sofa, but Samantha turns the gun back toward her, and she stops in her tracks.

"Scotch told Regina what?" My heart is hammering in my chest.

"That I pushed him that night at Lookout Point," Samantha says.

All is quiet as her confession washes over me.

"It was you?"

"Yes," she replies, her voice cracking.

"But why?"

She looks up at me pleadingly. "I did it for you, Vee. When you didn't come back right away, I started getting nervous. I wasn't sure you'd be able to handle Scotch on your own. We both know what he was capable of. So I came to see what was going on. You and Scotch were wrestling with each other at the edge of the cliff. And . . . I pushed him."

I stare at her with wide eyes.

She pushed Scotch? For *me*?

"I just kept thinking about Homecoming," Samantha says. "How I stood there and watched him drag you away.

And I didn't do anything. I couldn't let him hurt you again."

"Samantha," I say, reaching toward her. Rollins keeps me from going any farther.

"I'm so tired," Samantha says, squeezing her eyes shut. Her head lolls against her chest. "I just want to go to sleep."

While Samantha's head is down, Rollins breaks away from me and Mattie and circles the room, moving closer to Samantha. His muscles tense, and I think he's going to jump on her.

"Don't," I say.

Samantha's head snaps up. When she sees that Rollins is only a few feet away from her, she raises the gun in his direction.

"No!" I scream.

Confused, she turns toward me.

Rollins uses that moment to lunge at her. He pushes her onto the floor. The gun flies out of her hand and bounces on the white carpet.

A deafening sound.

I crouch down, covering my ears with my hands.

Mattie screams.

I straighten up and see Mattie pointing at Rollins. He's next to Samantha, who is crying quietly on the floor.

"Rollins? Rollins, are you okay?"

He doesn't answer.

I kick the gun far away from Samantha and run to Rollins's side. Grabbing his arm, I flip him over so he's facing me. His eyes are open. He doesn't look like he's breathing.

"Rollins, talk to me."

I throw open his leather jacket, looking for the wound. A red stain is blooming from the top of his right shoulder. There's so much blood. I pull off my hoodie and press it to Rollins's chest.

No, no. This can't be happening.

Regina is on the phone. I hear her talking, but I can't make sense of the words. Mattie has her hand over her mouth.

I drop my mouth to Rollins's ear.

Two words.

"Don't go."

CHAPTER THIRTY-TWO

I'm not much for prayer.

That's always been Mattie's thing.

But sitting in the waiting room at the hospital, I wish very hard.

I wish that Rollins being a good guy counts for something.

I wish that whoever's keeping score tallies up all the selfless things he's done in his life and sees that it's just not fair to take him away so soon.

Too bad I know better.

Life isn't fair.

And death certainly isn't.

I watch people coming and going all day long. A lot of them are sad, but there's a lot of laughter, too. You'd be surprised how much laughter there is in the hospital. I guess even when people are scared they're going to lose what's most important to them, they need to celebrate what they still have.

I still have a lot.

I've got Mattie.

She brings me coffee from the cafeteria and a tooth-brush from the gift shop when it's time to go to sleep. I won't go home, so she helps me make a bed out of some of the uncomfortable chairs and gives me her sweater as a blanket. She sits by me then, as I try unsuccessfully to get some sleep.

I've got my father.

He didn't say much as I explained what happened, but when I was done, he wrapped his arms around me and sat there for a long time, just holding me. He talks to Rollins's doctors and translates the medicalese that I don't understand. He tries to sound positive, but he doesn't give me false hope because he believes that family and friends should have an accurate picture of how serious a situation is. That's part of what makes him a good doctor, I suppose.

I have so much, but all I want is Rollins. It's strange and ironic that the only person I want right now, the only person who can make me feel better, isn't here.

He's in an in-between place.

It's raining outside. I watch as the water streams down the window, almost as if to make up for the tears I'm not crying.

I can't cry.

I can't eat.

I can't *think*, especially not about what life will be like if my best friend doesn't pull through.

I won't think about that.

———

On the second day, Lydia walks in. She looks around, spots me and Mattie, and walks toward us.

"Hello, girls."

Mattie looks up from her copy of *Seventeen*. "Oh, hey. I think I'm going to run to the cafeteria to get a pop. Do you guys want anything?"

I shake my head. Lydia does the same.

Mattie gets up and leaves. Lydia sets down her purse and takes the empty seat. I fix my eyes on my sneakers.

"I suppose I owe you an apology," I say, remembering how I hinted that Lydia might have had something to do with Scotch's death.

"Don't worry about that now."

We sit silently for a few minutes.

"I want to tell you why I came back to Iowa City after all these years," Lydia says, playing with her sleeve.

I think it's a strange time and place to choose to come clean to me, but I'm up for anything that will take my mind off what's happening right now. "Okay."

Lydia takes a deep breath. "There was a baby," she finally says, so quietly I can barely make out her words.

"A baby? In California?" I picture the man she left behind. Did she leave a child as well?

"No. Not in California. When I was sixteen. After your father broke up with me to date your mother, I found solace in another man. He was older. Married."

"Jesus," I whisper.

"I . . . I couldn't get rid of it. But I didn't want anyone to know. So I left." She grabs a couple of tissues from her purse and blows her nose.

"I don't understand. Why did you decide to come back to Iowa if your kid is in California?"

Lydia dabs at her eyes. "She's not in California. She's here. I went away for the duration of the pregnancy. The man confessed the affair to his wife. She was furious, but they'd been trying to have a child for a long time. She made him a deal. If he agreed to never see me again, they would take the child and raise it as their own. That girl at the diner, Melody? She's my biological daughter."

My jaw drops as I take this in. Despite my discomfort with the idea of Lydia dating my father, I can't help but feel sorry for the pregnant teenager who felt she had to leave her family and then give away her child.

"So why did you come back now? You could have come back anytime over the years. You could have seen my mother before she . . ." My voice trails off.

"Believe me, I wish I did come back earlier. I was just so ashamed. The fact of the matter is that I got engaged this year. He's a wonderful man. Better than I deserve. But I just couldn't do it. I kept remembering the baby girl I left behind. That's why I came back. Guess I needed some closure before I could move on with the rest of my life, you could say."

Lydia reaches out to hold my hand.

I let her.

"I would do anything to go back and tell your mother how much I loved her. Our fight was so stupid, and we let it ruin us for way too long."

I think of how hard it would be to learn that a loved one died without ever knowing how you really felt about them.

I start to cry.

It's been three days.

Three days of camping out in the waiting room, drinking coffee from the nurses' station, and flipping through the same old magazines.

Three days of watching people get good news and bad news, breaking into tears either way.

Three days of no news about Rollins.

Mattie snores in the chair next to me.

My father walks into the waiting room.

He.

Is.

Smiling.

A moment ago, my heart was in a million pieces, and I was pretty sure I'd never have the strength to assemble it again. Even though I don't really believe in a god, I was begging whoever was out there to please give me a chance to say good-bye to my best friend. I wanted to hold his hand and feel the pulse beneath his skin, just one more time.

But now.

My father is smiling.

I open my mouth, and a strangled sound escapes. Adrenaline pours through my veins, and I leap to my feet. I turn, finding Mattie, who is jumping up and down. We crash into a hug, and I start sobbing.

Now I can cry.

"Can I see him?" I beg my father.

He puts his hands on my shoulders. "Yes. He's still very groggy, but you can see him."

Following him back to Rollins's room, I can't stop grinning through my tears.

I will never stop.

The door is ajar, and I push it open the rest of the way. It smells like medicine and blood and survival.

Rollins is pale, his lips almost colorless. They took the lip ring out, and he looks naked without it. His eyes are closed, but his chest is rising and falling. I've never seen anything more beautiful.

I'm wrong, though, because then he opens his brown eyes and sees me standing there, and his lips curve into a smile. It takes my breath away.

"Hey, you," he says weakly.

I want to rush forward and press my lips against his and then kiss his eyelids and the warm spot just behind his ears, but I'm afraid I'll disturb the cords that poke out from his body. So I just step closer and take his hand.

There's a lot of things I want to say right now, but they all seem too serious and morbid. Instead, I look at his chest, which is wrapped in bandages. "Does it hurt?"

"Nah. They've got me on some pretty decent drugs. Your dad hooked me up."

I force a laugh. "That's good." My pathetic attempt at laughter turns into a sob.

"Hey," Rollins says softly. "Come here."

He pulls me into a hug. I'm careful to avoid pressing against his wound.

"I'm so glad you're okay," I whisper. The words don't seem like enough. They don't express what I really mean to say. Finally I figure it out, and I say the right words.

"I love you."

Rollins traces his finger along my jaw and brings me close for a kiss. It is soft and gentle and perfect.

"I love you, too."

CHAPTER THIRTY-THREE

I stand on Samantha's doorstep, holding a bouquet of daffodils. It's been a week since I stood in this exact same place, a week since Samantha was arrested for the murder of Scott Becker and the attempted murder of Rollins. I heard her parents had to rush home from Barbados to post an exorbitant amount of money for her bail. I guess she was lucky they let her come home at all.

The door opens a crack. Samantha's mother, looking frazzled, peeks out at me. "Sylvia?" She studies me warily. "What can I do for you?"

"I was hoping I could come in, Mrs. Phillips. I brought these for Samantha." I hold up the bouquet of flowers, in case the woman hadn't noticed them before.

"I'm very sorry, Sylvia. But Samantha doesn't want to see anyone." Mrs. Phillips starts to close the door.

"Please," I say. "I'd really like to speak to her."

The blond woman looks behind her and then back at me. Finally she seems to make up her mind and steps back. "Okay. But just for a minute."

I follow Mrs. Phillips up the stairs. When we pass through the living room, I try to avoid looking at the bloodstain that is still on the carpet.

"She's in her bedroom," says Mrs. Phillips, walking into the kitchen. "You know where it is."

"Thank you," I tell her, and then I make my way down the hallway to Samantha's room. I knock on the door. All is quiet. I knock again.

The door opens.

"Vee," Samantha whispers.

She looks like shit.

I hand her the bouquet of flowers. She accepts them, looking confused. "Why did you bring these?" She clutches them to her chest, searching my eyes for answers.

I shrug. "Because they're pretty. And I know you can't go outside."

We both look down at the electronic anklet on her leg.

"Can I sit down?"

She nods.

I cross the room and sit gingerly on her bed. Still holding the daffodils close, Samantha follows me and sits down.

"Is Rollins okay?" She avoids my gaze.

"Yeah. He's going to be just fine."

"I'm glad. You know I didn't mean to—"

"I know," I say, reaching out to touch her hand. "I know."

We sit still for a moment, both staring at the flowers.

I've spent a lot of time thinking about what could make a person do what Samantha did. I never in a million years would have thought she was capable of killing someone. But when I think about everything that led up to it, I guess I have a better understanding of her actions.

It was like a snowball, coming down the mountain. First, Scotch stole her panties and made up a nasty story about her. In retaliation, we planned to get him naked and leave him at Lookout Point. When she saw me fighting with him at the edge of the cliff, her emotions went out of control, and that's when she pushed him—not meaning to hurt him, but just to get him off me.

And then she must have been terrified. She tried to cover up her actions by sneaking back to the car and then pretending not to know what happened to Scotch. She thought she'd get in trouble if anyone found out. I mean, I know how she was feeling. I was scared, too.

"Do you want to talk about it?" I ask.

She lifts the flowers to her nose and inhales. "Okay."

"I understand everything you did," I say. "Up until the point you got to the hospital. I just didn't think you were capable of . . . killing someone."

She looks over at me and gives me a sad smile. "I didn't think I was, either. But I guess we were wrong."

She stands up, walks over to her desk, and dumps the pens and pencils out of a University of Iowa cup. As she starts to arrange the flowers, she speaks. "When I heard that Scotch woke up, I freaked out. I came home, and I was all by myself. I couldn't stop shaking. I just kept thinking about what would happen to me when Scotch told everyone that I pushed him. How my parents would hate me. How everyone would hate me."

"No one would have hated you," I say. "Not if you explained what happened."

Samantha stops fiddling with the flowers and raises an eyebrow at me. "Really? You don't think people would whisper things behind my back for the rest of high school? It would be like the rumor about me and Scotch hooking up, only ten thousand times worse. It would be never-ending."

"Okay, probably people would talk, but I still don't get how you thought it would be a good idea to go to the hospital and kill Scotch. I mean, how did you even come up with that?"

Samantha leans against the desk. "The idea wasn't to kill Scotch. I just wanted to scare him a little. I found some of my mom's old scrubs that she wears to bed sometimes. I put them on and went to the hospital and waited for the shift change. Then I snuck into Scotch's room. I just stood there for a little while, watching him. But then he woke up, and when he saw me, he started to yell. I panicked. I grabbed a pillow and stuffed it over his face."

"But how . . . I mean, he was so much bigger than you."

She shrugs. "A combination of him being weak and my adrenaline, I guess. I didn't mean to kill him. I just wanted him to shut up. When he stopped thrashing around, I took the pillow away, and he was just gone. So I ran."

I close my eyes and shake my head. Samantha didn't

mean to kill Scotch. I knew it all along. She was just terrified. She wanted him to be quiet. And she didn't know her own strength.

When she starts talking again, I open my eyes.

"I came home afterward and wrote a suicide note. I couldn't bear to face my parents after what I'd done. The plan was to use my father's gun, but Regina interrupted me. She came over, accusing me of killing Scotch to cover up our prank. We started fighting, and that's when Mattie called."

Samantha covers her mouth. "I really didn't mean to hurt anyone," she repeats. "It just happened."

I rise and go to her.

"I'm sorry," she sobs. "I'm so sorry."

I reply by hugging her hard.

We stand there for a while, until Samantha's mom comes and tells me it's time to leave.

At dinner that night, Lydia makes an announcement.

"It's time for me to go back to California and face my demons."

"Your demons, meaning your fiancé?" my father asks, barely keeping a straight face. He passes the green beans across the table to Mattie.

"My demons, meaning my fear of commitment. I'm going to take my sorry ass back to California and see if James will forgive me."

"What brought you to that decision?" I ask.

246

"You did," Lydia says, smiling.

"How so?"

"Well, I watched you forgive Samantha after she very nearly took away the thing most precious to you in this world. It gives me hope that James might do the same for me."

My father reaches across the table and rubs my arm. "She is pretty amazing, isn't she?"

"That she is."

I return Lydia's grin and realize, for the first time, how nice it is to have an aunt around, particularly one that looks almost identical to my mother.

That night on my way to the bathroom, I pass Mattie's open door. Lydia is inside the room, her suitcase open on the bed.

"Need any help?" I ask.

She turns around, a pair of jeans in her hands. She folds them into a haphazard square and then stuffs them into her bag. "Nope, I think I've got it covered."

She sits down on the bed and pats the spot next to her. "I have some things I think I should tell you before I leave."

I search her face, wondering what she wants to talk about. I take a seat beside her, waiting.

"So . . . Mattie told me pretty much everything about the last few weeks."

"Everything?" I ask, feeling embarrassed about how convinced I was that she was up to something terrible.

"Yes."

"*Everything* everything?"

She nods. "If you're referring to a particular trait you and Mattie inherited from your mother, then yes, she told me everything."

I suck in my breath.

"My mother . . . she was like us?"

Lydia smiles. "She was gifted, just like you girls."

"And this gift, do you have it?"

She chuckles. "I'm happy to say that gene passed me by."

I draw on the carpet with my toes. There's just one thing I've been wondering about, a question that's never been answered.

"If you don't mind my asking, why did you change your name to Lila Harrington?"

Lydia smoothes a wrinkle in her slacks. "It's hard to explain. After Melody's father brought her back to Iowa, I went through a period of depression. I was in so much pain whenever I thought about giving away my daughter. I wanted to start anew, I guess, and it seemed logical to start with a new name."

"Does James know about all of this?" I know very well he doesn't, but I want to hear her explain why she never told him.

"Like I said, I wanted a new life. I wasn't sure he'd want to begin a family with a woman who once gave away her own daughter. I wanted to pretend that this time was for real. But the night before our wedding, I realized I couldn't marry him—not until I'd sorted everything out at home."

I think about this. It makes sense that she'd want to wait

until she could be completely honest with James before they got married.

"I hope everything works out for you," I say, and I realize that I mean it.

"Me too," Lydia says, squeezing my shoulder.

CHAPTER THIRTY-FOUR

Diane Acton's house is small and tidy. There are pink impatiens planted around the tree in her front yard. The blue station wagon is parked in the driveway, looking much less sinister than it seemed when it was driving by my house.

"Do you want me to come in with you guys?" Rollins asks, subconsciously touching his chest. It's been weeks since he got out of the hospital, but he still feels quite a bit of pain where the bullet hit him.

I'm about to say no, but then I change my mind. I have a tendency to get myself into some pretty crazy situations. "That'd probably be best."

Mattie, Rollins, and I get out of the car and cross the lawn. A small dog yaps at us from across the street. We crowd onto the front step, and I ring the doorbell.

The door swings open, and Diane peeks out. Her mouth drops open when she sees me. "Sylvia? What are you doing here?"

I put my hands on my hips. "So you do remember me."

"Of course I remember. What do you need?"

"I have some questions I'm hoping you can answer for me. Can we come in?"

Diane nods. "Of course."

She holds open the door, and we all walk into her house. She leads us into the living room and gestures to a couch. "Would you like anything to drink?"

I shake my head and sit down. Mattie and Rollins sit on either side of me.

"Is this your sister?" Diane asks, sitting in a rocking chair on the other side of the room. "I can see the resemblance."

"Yes, this is Mattie. And this," I say, pointing, "is Rollins."

Diane raises her eyebrows. "I've never met anyone named Rollins before."

I ignore her comment and jump right in. "Why are you following me?"

"I beg your pardon?"

"I don't believe it was a coincidence that you were driving along Highway 6 the night I got into an accident. I never told you my address, but you knew how to get there anyway. And since then I've seen you watching me at the mall and driving by our house. Don't try to deny it, Diane."

"I won't," she says.

"Why were you following me?"

She pushes out of the rocking chair, steadies herself. I

feel Rollins tense beside me. I put my hand on his knee. It's not like this old woman is going to attack me. At least, I don't think she is.

Wordlessly, she walks out of the room. A moment later, she returns carrying two stuffed animals in her arms. One is a turtle with a missing eye. The other is a sheep. She gives the turtle to me, the sheep to Mattie.

A flurry of memories rushes through me. I haven't thought of this turtle in ages, but now that I'm holding it in my hands, I wonder how I ever could have forgotten it.

"Slowpoke," I say, calling it by its name. I look up at Diane, who has returned to the rocking chair. "How did you get this?"

"Your mother gave it to me."

I exchange an incredulous look with Mattie. "Are you serious? I mean, I know you knew our mom, but why would she give you our things?"

"Let me start at the beginning. Susan and I met at the hospital. She'd come by to bring your father lunch, and we just got to talking. After that, we were fast friends. I realized we had a lot in common."

Mattie speaks up. "Like what?"

Diane looks carefully at Rollins. "Would you mind excusing us, dear? This is private business."

"Anything you say to me, you can say in front of Rollins. There are no secrets between us," I tell her.

She straightens her skirt. "Okay, then. Susan, like me, had the gift of extraordinary empathy."

"Extraordinary what?" Mattie asks.

"Empathy is the ability to experience the feelings of another—"

I cut her off. "Is that what you call it? Extraordinary empathy?"

Diane studies me. "Well, that's what it is, isn't it? The capacity to literally walk in someone else's shoes?"

I gasp. "You're able to sl—to walk in someone else's shoes?"

A wry smile spreads across her lips. "My dear, I've walked in your shoes. Or should I say your bare feet?"

I wonder what she's talking about, and then I remember the night I got into the car accident. There was a moment, right before Scotch came down the road, I kind of blacked out. I thought it was because I was so disoriented from the car crash, but maybe this woman slid into me. I look at the stuffed animal in my hands. I'd loved it so much when I was small. Surely there was enough of an emotional imprint attached for Diane to use and find me.

"That night of the accident," I say.

She nods.

"But why?"

"I made a promise to your mother before she died. She came here shortly after she was diagnosed with cancer, and she made me promise to watch over you and Mattie. That's why she gave me the stuffed animals. In case I ever needed to . . . tap into you. I never thought I'd actually have to use them. But when I read in the papers about what happened with your friend Zane, I started to get nervous."

Hearing Zane's name is like a stab to the heart. I shake it off, try to concentrate on what Diane's saying.

She goes on. "I started following you periodically. One night, I happened to pass by your house. Vee, I saw you backing out of the driveway in your father's car. I'd never seen you driving before. I suspected it was because of your condition. So it was very odd to see you behind the wheel. I wanted to follow you, but I was nearly out of gas. I had to stop, and then I had no idea where you'd gone. That was the first night I used the turtle. I wanted to make sure you were okay. When I tapped into you, I saw that you were stranded on the side of the road."

"And then you came to pick me up," I said.

She nods.

Rollins speaks up.

"Are there more people like you and Vee and Mattie? Others with . . . extraordinary empathy?"

"Not many, but there are a few I've come across in my lifetime."

"Can we meet them? I have so many questions," says Mattie.

I realize that I have a lot of questions myself. Like, how was Mattie able to control people so easily, while I had to work up to it? Why does she slide only when she's asleep? Is sliding from a waking state something you work up to?

"If that's what you want," says Diane. "It's probably hard for you, without anyone to talk to about your ability. I could get in touch with one or two of them. And, in the meantime, you can always talk to me."

"I'd like that," I say.

I run my fingers through the turtle's soft fur, thinking how glad I am to have found others who are able to do what I can do. For so long, I felt alone, but now I have someone to guide me.

I look at Mattie and smile.

And someone to share my journey.

CHAPTER THIRTY-FIVE

The doorbell rings.

"Vee? Can you get that?"

My dad stands in the living room, fumbling with his video camera. You'd think a pediatric surgeon would be able to master the fundamentals of making a home movie, but he keeps forgetting where the zoom button is.

"Sure."

I open the door, revealing a tuxedo-clad Russ shuffling his feet and holding a plastic container with a white rose corsage in front of him. He looks adorably nervous.

"Is Mattie ready?"

"Almost. Would you like to come in?"

He tugs at his collar. "Sure."

My father, Russ, and I wait in the living room for Mattie to come downstairs. "Here she comes, Miss America," my father booms when she appears.

"*Dad,*" Mattie says, but she's smiling. She looks drop-dead gorgeous in her strapless red dress. It's kind of a shock to see her looking so mature, even though I know she's grown up a lot this past year. My father must be having the same thoughts because his broad grin falters just a little. He covers it up with his camera and starts filming.

Mattie picks up her skirt so it won't trip her on the way downstairs. At the bottom, Russ meets her with the rose. He nervously pins it to her dress. "Ow," Mattie says, and when Russ gives her a mortified glance, she says, "Just kidding."

They start for the door, but my father stops them. "Wait a second. I promised Lydia she'd get to see you before you left."

Mattie turns around and tries to look irritated, but it's obvious she's loving every minute of the whole production. She guides Russ into my father's office, and they get my aunt on Skype. I hang back in the doorway, watching.

"Ohmigod, you two look amazing," Lydia shrieks, clapping her hands together. She stops and cranes her neck, seeming to look for someone. "Where's Rollins?"

Mattie glances back at me. "They're too cool for prom," she says sarcastically. This has been a point of contention between us. Mattie begged me to go, but I just won't do it. I still have a bad taste in my mouth from wearing that stupid pink tank top and miniskirt to the movie a few weeks ago. I've decided never to go against my instincts again, and my intuition is saying that prom sucks.

"We're going to stay home and watch *Carrie* tonight."

Lydia pouts. "You're no fun." She turns her attention

back to Mattie. "Have fun at the dance, sweetie."

"We will!" Mattie takes Russ's arm, and they push past me.

"Be safe!" my father says. "Remember, your curfew is two."

"Wow," Lydia comments. "You've loosened up on your rules since I was there."

My father puts his arm around my shoulders. "I've got some good girls."

Lydia cocks her head and smiles. "You sure do."

"Vee!" Mattie yells from the foyer. "Rollins is here."

"Have fun," Lydia tells me.

"Talk to you later, Lydia," I reply. We've been Skyping a couple times a week since she went back to California. She's planning to visit us again this summer, but this time she's bringing her fiancé.

By the time I get to the front door, Mattie and Russ have already left. Rollins stands waiting for me, his hands in the pockets of his faded jeans. Underneath his vintage Led Zeppelin T-shirt, I can see the outline of his bandage.

"We could still go if you changed your mind," Rollins says, looking a little concerned. "I know how you love hanging out in a stinky gymnasium and sipping bad punch."

"I think I'll survive," I say, wrapping my arms around his waist and looking up into his eyes.

He flinches, and I worry that I squeezed him too tightly.

"Are you okay?"

"Ha, yeah, I was just playing with you. Hey, do you have a radio around here?"

Wondering why he wants a radio, I nod. "Yeah. It's in the kitchen. Why?"

"Because Anna is on tonight, and she's going to do something for me."

I pull away from him. "Uh, okay." Sinking into one of the chairs, I point toward the radio on top of the counter. "There it is."

Rollins bends down and fiddles with the knobs until he finds KRNK. There's an old Alanis Morissette song playing. He looks around. "Do you know what time it is?"

I glance at the clock on the stove. "Two minutes until seven."

"Great." He leans against the counter and nods along as Alanis sings about scratching her nails down some dude's back. I slouch in my chair, frowning.

"The movie's going to start any minute now," I say.

"Shhhhh," he says. "The song's over. Listen."

Anna's voice comes on. "Well, folks, it looks like it's seven o'clock, which means it's time for me to honor a very special request. This one goes out from Rollins to Vee. He says, 'Even though we're not at prom, can I have this dance?' Go for it, Rollins."

Astonished, I look at Rollins. He planned this? For me?

The song starts off soft, then gets louder. I recognize it from his first night on the radio. The one that, to him, screams true romance—"Everlong" by Foo Fighters.

Rollins pushes away from the counter. "Well, can I? Have this dance?"

He holds out his hand, and I let him pull me to my feet.

"This is kind of a hard song to dance to," I say, laughing.

"Then just hold me," he says dramatically, pulling me close. I hug him, careful not to put too much pressure on his wound. We sway back and forth, listening to the music. Rollins buries his face in my hair. I can feel his lips moving as he mouths along with the lyrics. He moves one hand under my hair, to the base of my neck.

"What's this?" he asks.

Not sure what he's talking about, I look down. He's holding the necklace made out of my mother's wedding diamond. I struggled with the idea of wearing it because I still don't want to slide into Lydia, but I switched the chain and am careful to keep the stone from touching my skin. It makes me feel closer to my mother, wherever she is.

"It reminds me of her," I say simply.

I don't have to say who. That's the great thing about me and Rollins: We never have to explain ourselves. It's funny—after Zane, I wasn't sure I could trust anyone again. Zane made me doubt my own feelings. Was it really love? Did that even exist? But then I realized that the problem was that Zane and I didn't even really know each other. It was insta-love, totally fleeting. We bonded over our losses, and we experienced something intense, but it wasn't real.

Rollins and I, on the other hand, have built our relationship on something solid—the truth. He knows everything there is to know about me, and I'm learning more about him every day.

We are best friends, but we are so much more.

Rollins lowers his face to mine. Our lips meet.

And I know this is for real.

ACKNOWLEDGMENTS

Thanks to:

Donna Bray, for helping me piece together the puzzle (so much fun!).

Sarah Davies, whose support I am beyond lucky to have and who is always there when I freak out about something dumb.

Julia Churchill, for sending me a YouTube video of tiny baby gerbils taking a bath when I was having a bad day.

Noukka Signe, for a stunning photograph, and Alison Klapthor, for designing another beauty. Yay, pink!

Brenna Franzitta, Emilie Polster, Caroline Sun, Viana Siniscalchi, and everyone at Balzer + Bray and HarperCollins, I kiss you!

Megan Miranda, with whom I can easily exchange fifty emails a day, debating important topics like whether we should have mac 'n' cheese for lunch or just some Fritos. Oh, and sometimes we critique each other's work. *fist bump*

My husband, for boosting me up and never letting me down. I love you like our son loves Lil' Crunchies.

My daughter, whose chest puffs up every time she spots "Mommy's books" at a store or on a shelf. Maybe someday she'll be old enough to read one of those books.

My son, who forced me to consume half a zillion Oreos while I simultaneously grew him in my belly and wrote this book.

My mother, for hating all the people I wanted her to hate (in my books, I swear). And, ya know, for being awesome in general.

My father, who says my books rock.

My sister, for being my biggest fan.

My brothers, for going into a career that will forever provide me with new story ideas.

My in-laws, for being pretty much amazing in every way. Thanks for all the help you've given us over the years.

My students, for inspiring me to write stories that teens will *want* to read.

My *former* teachers, who taught me that it's improper to call them my *old* teachers. I'm sure I'll appreciate that in a couple of years.

Officer Teahen, for letting me again borrow his name. I hope you enjoy this one.

My Secret Sliders, who tweeted and Facebooked and blogged about *Slide* until their fingers probably almost fell off. And especially those who were so enthusiastic about my *Slide* Day shenanigans (you know who you are).

Diet Pepsi. You are the devil, but I still love you.